THE PRINCESS OF WINDSWEPT

ARIEL LUCAS

THE PRINCESS OF WINDSWEPT
Copyright © 2016 by Ariel Lucas

All rights reserved. Except for the use in any review, the reproduction or utilization of this work in whole or in part in any form by an electronic, mechanical or other means, now known or hereinafter invented, including xerography, photocopying and recording, or in any information storage or retrieval system, is forbidden without the written permission of the publisher.

This is a work of fiction. Names, characters, places and incidents are either the product of the author's imagination or are used fictitiously, and any resemblance to actual persons, living or dead, business establishments, events or locales is entirely coincidental.

Edited by Amber Harrelson-Williams

Cover Model Megan Kuhar

Cover Photo by Todd Kuhar

Cover Design and Formatting by Mallory Rock

To all those who are chosen...
you are stronger than you know

Chapter 1

"It was just a kiss."

I could barely get the words out. I was so stunned that my voice sounded like it was coming from another part of the room. I watched as my mom, still dressed in her designer business suit and heels, dragged my suitcases from under the bed and started hauling my clothes out of the closet.

"Mom, you can't do this. Please." I felt like my whole body was melting. This couldn't be happening.

"Oh, yes I can do this. It is already done." Her tone was final and biting, her mouth clenched shut in an angry straight line. My mind raced for something to say, but before I could think of anything she whirled around and glared at me. I saw the lecture coming.

"There's no such thing as 'just a kiss,' Danni. Not at your age. I can't be with you 24/7 to control what you do with your friends at the mall, but I definitely have the power to remove you from the situation. Your flight leaves at 6:45 in the morning and you *will* be on it. Randall will have to take you to the airport because I can't miss work. I've already talked to your grandfather. He'll pick you up in Atlanta."

I still couldn't think of anything to say. I wanted to lash out at her – scream – but I was too hurt. She made it sound like I had done something terrible. If only my dad were still alive none of this would be happening. I fought back tears because I didn't want to give her the satisfaction of seeing me cry. I swallowed hard and tried to steady my voice.

"We were just goofing off, being silly, Mom. It's what teenagers do. It didn't mean anything."

And then she said it – that age-old parental failsafe. "This is for your own good, Danni. You'll thank me someday. Now finish packing. We'll box up anything that you can't get into the suitcases and send it to you later."

And just like that she left my room. Case closed, end of discussion. She had waltzed in, ruined my life and now I had to deal with it.

I must have sat there for an hour trying to process everything that had happened. The day had started off like any other except that I had spent an unusual amount of time in the bathroom admiring my perfectly straight teeth. The last two days without metal in my mouth had been wonderful.

My best friend, Kim, and I had planned a fun day to celebrate. I had been saving my money all summer, and we were going to the mall to look for new school clothes and then to Carmen's Caramel Shop at the food court. Caramel corn was number one on my list of things to eat after I got my braces off.

We had a great time. It was always fun to shop with Kim. She wanted to be a fashion designer, and could put the cutest outfits together for almost nothing. By lunchtime we were both famished. We were standing in line at Carmen's when Kim started waving at someone. At first I didn't see who it was and then I realized that Jack Corbin was strolling toward us.

Jack Corbin was without a doubt the most popular guy at school last year. His family had moved to LA from Australia a year earlier and he had become an instant celebrity at Commerce High. He was a movie star in the making with sandy blonde hair that curled perfectly around his handsome face. He was lean, tan, and athletic with a surfer's physique. Jack Corbin was a total Prince Charming with a delicious Australian accent.

I had no idea that Kim even knew him, but Kim was like that. She seemed to know everyone. Unlike me, she was very confident and outgoing and could fit in comfortably no matter where she was or who she was with. She had the ability to move in and out of all the tricky little cliques at school with ease. Everyone liked her. We met in Freshman Biology when we were paired for an experiment and had been best friends ever since.

And now Jack Corbin was walking toward us.

"Hi Jack!" Kim called out quite naturally. I just stood there frozen.

Jack's smile dazzled. "Hi yourself!" Kim seemed unaffected, but I felt weak at the knees when he nodded in my direction.

"Have you met Danni?"

"Not officially. No. But you go to Commerce, right? I've seen you around."

I nodded. Unable to speak. I couldn't believe that he even knew that I existed. He glanced at the caramel corn display.

"Ah, Carmen's. It's the best."

Thank goodness for Kim. She didn't miss a beat.

"We are celebrating. Danni just got her braces off. Show him that picture perfect smile, girl."

I tried to manage a smile that showed my teeth, but it felt more like a grimace. I must have looked like an idiot, but if I did, he didn't let on.

"Nice. Very nice. I remember getting mine off a couple of years ago. It was such a relief. But I still have to wear the retainer." I was surprised. It was hard to imagine Jack Corbin doing normal human things like putting in a retainer.

And then it happened. Kim suddenly grabbed my bags and pushed me toward Jack. "I know, let's get a picture to commemorate the occasion." I started to protest, but Jack just laughed good-naturedly and put his arm around my waist.

"Sure. I'll have my picture taken with a pretty girl any day." I think he actually meant me. Kim had fished out her phone and was lining up the shot.

"You should just give her a kiss, Jack!" And that's how it had happened. In one quick move Jack Corbin had spun me around in an elaborate Hollywood-style maneuver and tilted me backward.

I had never kissed a boy before, but it was everything that I had always dreamed a kiss would be. Cradled in his strong arms, his lips warm and gentle on mine. It was one of those moments that seem to happen in slow motion, but in reality was over in a few seconds.

Several people at nearby tables applauded, and I must have turned ten shades of red. Jack laughed, leaned close and whispered, "Thanks. That was nice," as he steadied me and then waved dashingly to his food court audience. Then everything seemed to go back to normal. Jack stepped away.

"Look, I've got to go find my little brother. He's running around here somewhere unattended. Mum will kill me. I'll see you at school, I guess. I can't believe it starts next week."

He winked at me as he walked away.

"See ya, Jack." Kim said distractedly. I panicked when I realized that she was already uploading the photo. I forgot about Jack and tried to get the phone.

"Kim, don't!" But it was too late. I grabbed her phone to look. It was actually a really great picture –

very romantic. She had captured the perfect moment when our lips touched. I almost didn't recognize myself. A pretty girl with long hair floating off her shoulders was kissing Jack Corbin – and it was me!

Two hours later the picture had been liked over 89 times and had twenty-two comments. Only seven people had dissed the photo – mostly jealous girls who made rude remarks about how Jack Corbin could do a lot better than me.

Sitting in my room now with my clothes in big heaps on the bed, it all seemed like a dream. I was still surprised that he had kissed me. I closed my eyes for a moment and relived the touch of his lips and the strength of his body next to mine. It had been a first-kiss fairytale moment that my mother had turned into something awful and embarrassing.

How was I ever going to tell Kim? I didn't know what to say. Finally I just texted her the truth.

> Mom is really mad about the picture.

Kim's reply came back in seconds.

> Seriously?
> She's sending me to stay with granddad.
> NO!
> Ticket is on my dresser.
> Don't they live on the other side of the country?
> Yes.
> In the middle of nowhere?
> Kind of.
> I'll come over and explain. It's my fault.

> No don't. She's really mad. It will just make it worse.
>
> What can I do?
>
> I don't know. Maybe she'll change her mind.
>
> This can't be happening. School starts next week.
>
> I know.
>
> Have you heard from Jack?
>
> No, you?

I hadn't even thought about how all this publicity might be affecting him. My face flushed red in embarrassment. He probably regretted that the kiss ever happened.

> Yeah. He loved the picture. Thought you were nice.
>
> Really? He's not mad?
>
> No, but he'll be upset when he hears about this.
>
> Please don't say anything. Please.
>
> I won't. I'm so sorry.
>
> It's okay. I've got to go.
>
> Call me later?
>
> Okay.

I stood up stiffly. I didn't know where to start. I kept thinking that Mom would come back in and tell me that it was all a big mistake, but instead, my half-sister Mariela came pushing through my door with a big box which she promptly threw on the floor.

"Mom wanted me to make sure that you were packing. Here's a box."

I was still at a loss for words. I just looked at her. Mariela was about as close to visual perfection as possible. She was tall, thin, and perfectly proportioned with five different shades of blonde highlights framing her stunning face, and if my mother had her way, Mariela was going to be a star. She was only seventeen, but there was something calculated about her beauty that gave her the look of someone much older. Maybe it was the severe arch of her meticulously tweezed brows or just too much shading under the cheekbones. Whatever it was added to the haughtiness she always seemed to project. And there was certainly no sympathy coming from her now. She just stood there like she was expecting me to apologize or something.

We had never been close. I had always known that she was Mom's favorite. Mariela was Mom's daughter by her first boyfriend. She had been madly in love with him, but he took off when she got pregnant. My dad had swooped in like a knight in shining armor a year later when Mariela was just a baby and they were married. I had been born two years after that, but even in my earliest memories I was aware that Dad and I would always come in second where Mariela was concerned.

Dad had always tried to make it up to me, but he was in the military and had to be away a lot. When he was home though, he was the greatest dad in the world. I always felt like a princess when he was in the room. He had tried so hard to be a dad to Mariela, too, but she didn't want anything to do with him. It was almost like she was afraid that allowing him in would require her to relinquish the power she had over Mom, so she would just watch jealously as he and I played together.

"Really, Danni, what were you thinking? You brought this on yourself."

Looking at her now, I recognized the expression on her face and I felt like I had been kicked in the stomach. It was the same expression she used to have when she would watch Dad and me together. My mouth went dry and I felt myself tremble with anger. In that instant I knew with certainty that I wasn't being sent away because Mom was mad about the kiss or even worried about me. I was being sent away because Mariela liked Jack Corbin.

It made perfect sense. They were both going to be seniors and they were both part of the high school in-crowd. Mariela had every intention of being Homecoming Queen, Prom Queen, and anything else she set her mind to. Jack Corbin was the natural choice to be her arm candy. The fact that he had kissed me in such a public way had really upset her plans.

"Oh, and you won't be needing this." She made her way past me and grabbed my phone and headed toward the door. "Mom says your grandfather will put you on his plan." And then she was gone, slamming the door as she left.

I couldn't hold back the tears one more second. I slipped to floor and sobbed. After my dad died, I had often felt like Cinderella. Although Mom and Mariela didn't lock me in a room, I was never included in their plans. I had learned early on that if I stayed out of their way, I could be reasonably happy and do my own thing. But now that I had kissed Jack Corbin, all that had changed. I was suddenly a threat to be dealt with.

I cried until I couldn't cry anymore. I cried because I missed my dad so much. I cried because I knew that Mom and Mariela didn't really care about me. I cried because I wouldn't get to say goodbye to my best friend. I cried because I was scared of leaving in the morning. And I cried because I wanted Jack Corbin to kiss me again and now that was never going to happen. Finally the tears stopped and I was just an empty heap on the floor.

For a second, I thought about running away, but I wasn't stupid. I was well aware of what happened to runaways on the streets of LA. Eventually I did the only thing I could do. I picked myself up and went to the bathroom to wash my face. I looked terrible. I was grateful for the numbness that had invaded me. It would make packing easier.

The clock on my nightstand winked 3:00 a.m. just as I finished zipping the suitcases. I knew that we would be leaving for the airport soon so it seemed pointless to try and sleep. I sat on the floor holding the most important thing I owned. It was a stuffed toy my dad bought me when I was nine. Dad was being deployed again, and before he left he presented me with a plain little brownish-yellow stuffed toy duckling with a pink ribbon around her neck. I loved the little brown duck immediately and named her Macaroni.

Macaroni was extra special because she had a secret pouch under her furry wing, and tucked safely inside was a rather ordinary looking key. The key was to be our secret. Dad said it was the key to his heart and that I would always be the one who owned it, and that if I ever needed it, I would know when to use it.

I didn't understand what he meant at the time, but in the years that have passed since then I have often wondered if he had sensed that he would not be coming home again, because that was the last time I saw him. To this day, no matter how alone I felt, I could always feel for the key and be reminded of how much he loved me.

I missed Dad so much right now that it physically hurt in the pit of my stomach. I was glad I had no more tears, but I still felt like I was wailing on the inside. I could hear movement upstairs and the aroma of coffee was drifting down the hallway from the kitchen. Mom had set the timer for an early start. I tucked Macaroni safely into my carry on. I wasn't going to let them see me defeated. I went ahead and pulled my luggage into the kitchen by the garage door.

Mom and Randall were surprised to see me sitting at the table when they came down. I actually felt sorry for Randall. He was the latest in a long line of inappropriate boyfriends my mom seemed to need.

Slightly younger than her, unemployed, and willing to play whatever role she needed. Today it was chauffeur. He grabbed his coffee and ducked out of the room quickly.

Mom avoided my gaze. "Have you had anything to eat?" Her tone seemed to imply that she was actually concerned about my well-being.

"I'm not hungry."

"Well, you should take a granola bar. It's going to be a long day. You know you have a lay-over in Dallas."

I didn't feel the need to answer – thankful again for the numbness I felt. There was a long silence broken only by the sound of her spoon stirring the coffee.

"Be sure to call me when you get there," she finally said.

"You took my phone." I said flatly. I could see that she had forgotten that little bit of hurtfulness, and now she was calculating her response – approaching this conversation like one of her strategy meetings at work. All that mattered to her was that she remained in control.

"Well, have your grandfather text me then." She sipped her coffee without looking at me.

Sitting there in the awkward silence, I realized that I was still harboring a faint glimmer of hope that she would change her mind. I was clinging to the possibility that she would feel she had punished me enough for the grave error of kissing Jack Corbin in a public place, and that she would, in a grand gesture of motherly benevolence, let me have my life back. In the back of my mind I could still see a chance for a normal sophomore year having fun with Kim.

She dashed all of that with her next words.

"I've already had your school records transferred. There shouldn't be any problem with your enrollment."

Her eyes met mine with a cool triumphant gaze just as Randall came barreling back into the room, his keys jangling. "We'd better get a move on if we are going to get you through security. I'll get these suitcases out to the car." Neither of us looked away as he walked between us to go to the door. It was Mariela who interrupted our stalemate. She bounced into the room looking ridiculously perfect so early in the morning.

"Oh, Danni, I was afraid you'd already left. I just wanted to say good-bye. I'll miss you." Mariela's voice was sugary sweet. Those acting lessons were paying off. If I hadn't known better, I might even have believed her caring big-sister act. But I knew it was performed solely for the benefit of our mother. Randall tapped on the car horn lightly in the garage. I stood up and headed for the door. I was wounded and drained, but I intended to have the last word. I turned to Mariela.

"Thanks, Mariela. Oh, and good luck with Jack Corbin. You are going to need it."

I had nailed it. The look on their faces confirmed everything. Mariela's eyes went wide with surprise and guilt. Her mouth fell open slightly. My mom actually stiffened and was temporarily at a loss for words, which almost never happened. I didn't give her time to think of a defense.

"See ya." I pulled the door shut behind me.

CHAPTER 2

The jolt of the plane woke me up. I must have dozed off out of sheer exhaustion. I had been grateful for the window seat on the second leg of the trip. The last thing I remembered was leaning my head against the cabin wall and looking down at the sea of clouds with the sun shining brightly on their white puffy waves. The brief sleep had only made me feel groggy and my head and neck ached. I quickly wiped a bit of drool from my cheek.

"Ladies and gentlemen, the captain has turned on the fasten seatbelt sign. At this time we ask that you return to your seat…"

I didn't listen to the rest. We were emerging from the clouds and the sprawling city of Atlanta was already visible below. I felt a lump in my throat. The last time I had been to this airport was for my dad's funeral. It seemed so long ago and far away. I realized I was nervous about seeing my granddad again, too. He had made every effort to stay in touch after Dad's death. He had even visited LA several times to see me, but Mom had made it known in her not-so-subtle way that he really wasn't wanted.

He had remarried two years ago and I had been invited to the wedding all expenses paid, but Mom would not let me attend. She used school as an excuse. My relationship with Granddad had dwindled to a phone call now and then, and a gift card several times a year. I felt guilty and embarrassed about being dropped back into his life like this.

I wondered how much Mom had told him about what happened. What could she possibly say? That I kissed a boy at the mall and had gone wild? It was humiliating. I wondered if Granddad's new wife, Myra, would be with him. My grandmother had passed away before I was born, so when I heard about the marriage, I was really glad for my granddad. He had been alone a long time and had been through too much sadness. That was something we had in common.

The walk up the corridor into the airport seemed to take forever. I searched the crowds ahead for a familiar face, trying to remember what Granddad looked like. I saw him before he saw me. He wasn't a tall, muscular man like my dad. He was slighter in build but still very handsome with just a touch of gray at the temples. When he saw me, he burst into a big smile that made me want to believe that everything was going to be okay.

I practically ran into his arms and clung to him for several minutes before I could let go. He hugged me tight and said, "Hey young'un. It's good to see you." I gulped and fought back tears. He must have sensed my despair because he kept hugging me. "I got you girl," he murmured. He finally stepped back and cupped my face in his hands. "You are a sight for sore eyes, young lady." He smiled and then kissed me on the forehead.

"Hey, Granddad." I swallowed hard, still fighting tears. "It's good to see you, too."

"What'd 'ya say we get your stuff and get out of here." He put his arm around my shoulder as we headed for the baggage claim. "Myra wanted to be here to meet you, but she's gone crazy fixin' up a room for you and she wanted to cook a big welcome dinner. Of course there's a whole cooler of snacks in the car, too. She wanted to make sure we could feed an army in case we met one on the road." He laughed and I could see that just talking about her made him happy. I found myself smiling, too.

It only took us about forty-five minutes to get out of the worst of the Atlanta traffic and soon we were sailing along with open country on either side of the car. Everything looked so foreign and…different. I could feel a wave of homesickness overtaking me.

And even though Granddad was being wonderful, it felt like there was a very large elephant in the back seat that we weren't talking about. I finally just blurted it out for the second time in twenty-four hours.

"It was just a kiss, Granddad. It wasn't anything bad. It was…my first." I felt my cheeks flush red.

Granddad smiled at me kindly.

"Well, leave it to that woman to turn your first kiss into something you'll have to go to therapy for later on in life."

His response completely shocked me, but when I looked at him, he winked at me and grinned. Suddenly we were both laughing. It felt good to know that someone else could see how absurd this situation was.

"Listen." Granddad reached across the seat and grabbed my hand. "Danni, I know this has to be hard for you. It's not where you want to be or how you would want things to be with your mom. Myra and I know that it's just a matter of time before she realizes that she's made a big mistake and sends for you – so we plan to make every moment that you are here count. Okay? I'm just looking forward to getting to know my granddaughter again."

"Thanks, Granddad. Me too." I felt like crying again, but I was relieved to hear that he thought Mom might change her mind. There was still hope. He squeezed my hand.

"Now this," he pointed to a green sign up ahead, "is our exit." As we got closer I could see that the sign read: Malvern, 42 miles.

The change in direction didn't make me feel any better. The two-lane road we were on now was curvy with lots of hills and dips. We had not passed a house or store in twenty minutes. I remembered what Kim said about this being in the middle of nowhere. I had an overwhelming sense of despair at being totally disconnected from everything I knew – as if I were slipping away into nothingness somehow. I was so relieved to see a gas station and a house a few minutes later.

"Now, if you turn left here, that road will take you to the plant where I work. Hadley Aerospace. Takes about 10 or 15 minutes to get there." I had forgotten that Granddad had a degree in engineering. "And the quickest way to get to the house is just to go straight for about ten minutes and turn right at Windmere Estates. You'll learn the lay of the land soon enough, but I want to take a little detour and show you the school." He gave his signal and turned down the second left.

I immediately wished that he hadn't. We passed a sign that said, "Welcome to Malvern, Population 1,890." I swallowed hard. There were almost that many people at my old high school.

"Quaint" would probably be a word that some people would use to describe Malvern, but I couldn't think of any adjective that would be so kind. It consisted of a couple of streets lined with small stores and eateries. The tiny downtown area gave way to a cross-hatch of streets lined with older looking homes.

"You turn right here to get to the elementary school, but up here on the left is the high school." My heart sank as we got closer. Several school buses were lined up in front of a very old three story brick building. A breezeway to the side connected the main building to a smaller, newer structure that had a lot of windows down its length. A large banner was hanging over the entrance that said "Welcome Back Mavericks!" Behind the two buildings, I could see the tops of stadium lights. It was hard to believe that the school was even big enough to have a football team.

"Your dad loved this school." Granddad's words were a shock and I felt ashamed. I hadn't even thought about my dad going here. "It's small, but the programs are top notch. They are some of the best in the state," he said proudly."Hadley has a scholarship program and a lot of students do internships and start work there right after college."

I felt bad but I couldn't think of anything to say. I was busy trying not to cry. This was just too much. My heart was all the way in the pit of my stomach now. The reality of the situation engulfed me. I made up my mind right then that I would call Mom the first chance I got and just beg. I would let Mariela win. I didn't care anymore. All I wanted to do was go home.

"And this turn," Granddad didn't seem to notice my silence, "will take us right back to Old 23 – which is what we were on after the exit."Granddad was so sweet, but I wanted to yell that I didn't care about the stupid school or where we were. I wanted to plead with him to take me back to the airport. Even he had said that he knew this was all a big mistake.

For a moment, I imagined Jack Corbin coming to rescue me. He would fly in by helicopter like in the movies and just as I was going to my first day of school, he would sweep me up while everyone watched and whisk me away from all of this. Maybe take me to Australia. I knew it was a silly fantasy, but it helped me get past my need to sob hysterically. In reality, Jack Corbin had probably already forgotten all about me and the kiss.

At least Windmere Estates turned out to be nice. It was a newly constructed subdivision on the outskirts of the town. The two-story houses all looked similar, but at least they were bright and clean and the yards were carefully landscaped. Granddad made several turns onto different streets before slowing down.

"Now just down there is the clubhouse for the development. It has a really nice pool and recreational center. This street we are on just makes a big loop back to the entrance. And this," he turned on his right blinker, "is our street. Windswept. Ours is the last house down there."

The street actually went downhill steeply and curved to the left. From our vantage point at the top, I could see that there were houses on either side until the big curve at the bottom. After that only two houses remained on the right side of the road. The development just abruptly came to an end. Behind the last two houses was a very large field and past that a huge stand of trees that went on as far as the eye could see.

There was nothing past Granddad's house but country. I truly was in the middle of nowhere.

I realized Granddad was waiting for me to say something. I managed to squeak out "It's very pretty," as he turned down the hill.

"Yeah, Myra picked it out," Granddad was smiling again. "She really liked the view. We had some trouble with ice on this hill last winter, but other than that we like calling it home. Some of these houses are still empty, but I think we'll get some more people moving in once the economy picks up."

Granddad went on to talk about one of the neighbors that had moved to Italy for two years, but I was distracted by a young girl playing in the yard of the house next to his. As we drove closer, I could see that she was probably only four years old. She was dancing around in a makeshift fairy princess costume – a dollar store tutu over her shorts with light up sneakers and a sparkly crown that was mashed down onto her unruly curls. She wore pink-rimmed glasses that she had to keep adjusting with one hand because they were sliding down her nose. With her other hand she was enchanting the air with a plastic wand. I had to smile. She was adorable.

When she saw our car she immediately stopped dancing and stood very still and looked at us. A worried little frown burrowed into her forehead. I smiled at her and she slowly raised her arm and wiggled her fingers in a very hesitant, odd sort of wave. I waved back.

I was going to ask Granddad about her, but at that moment a young man came striding out of the garage and I caught my breath. He was stunning to look at. He was maybe a couple years older than me. Not old enough to be the little girl's father. A brother maybe. He was dressed in black jeans and a black t-shirt that had colorful smudges on the front. He was tall with long dark hair that framed his face and grazed his shoulders. His face was gorgeous except that he had the same worried look as the little girl. Not a frown exactly, but an intensity that strained his forehead.

Our eyes met for a second and I actually felt electrified by his gaze. I looked away quickly, blushing at the idea of being caught staring at him. When I got up the nerve to glance back, he was already ushering the little girl into the house. His long hair shielded his face now, but the little girl was craning her neck to stare at our car, almost tripping as she went up the front steps.

I wanted to ask Granddad who they were, but he was already turning into his driveway next to another car and explaining that they weren't using the garage right now because Myra was using it for storage. I felt a pang of guilt. They probably had to rearrange their whole house in order to take me in on such short notice. I didn't have time to worry too much about it because Myra came running out the front door waving both hands and smiling. She was a short, plump lady with red hair and twinkling eyes. She had always seemed very nice on the phone.

"You're here! You're here!" She engulfed me in a warm, softly scented embrace as I got out of the car. "I can't tell you how happy I am!" She held me at arm's length and gave me a quick once over. "My goodness, you are even prettier in person if that is possible!"

"Thank you," I smiled weakly. It had just hit me how stiff, tired, and exhausted I felt. As if on cue, she wrapped her arm around my waist and steered me toward the door.

"Let's get you inside and get you something to eat. You must be exhausted. Don't worry about your luggage. We'll let your granddad get that. Let me give you a quick tour of the house and then you can get freshened up for dinner. I'll bet you haven't eaten all day."

She was right, and the delicious aroma that greeted us as we walked in was enough to make my stomach do interested flip flops. The house was very nice inside…everything carefully displayed and matching. It looked like it belonged in a designer magazine. I noticed there were several pictures of me on the mantle and one of Dad in his uniform, along with a wedding photo of Myra and Granddad.

"Now," she exclaimed after we had circled through the family areas and made our way back to the staircase at the entrance, "Your granddad and I sleep upstairs, and there are a couple of extra rooms up there. But we thought you might like to have a little privacy, so I hope the guest room down here will be okay." She headed down the hallway and I followed. "That's the den," she pointed to a closed door, "But this will be your room if you like it." She opened the door to a surprisingly spacious room at the back of the house. There were no windows, but the entire back wall was a sliding glass door that opened onto a large deck that overlooked the field and the woods in the distance. The floor-length drapes had been pushed back for full effect.

"This is so nice, Myra. Thank you. It's...it's lovely." I really meant it. Every effort had been made to make the room inviting and feminine. Myra was pleased.

"I know it's kind of sparse, but you can decorate it however you'd like. Make it your own. We can go shopping to get anything you need. Now, I've got to run and get the lasagna out so you just make yourself at home. We'll eat in about a half an hour if that is okay. Your granddad gets grumpy if he doesn't get his dinner on time." She whispered the last part and then laughed. She started to leave, but then turned back and gave me a concerned look. "Danni, this really is your home now for as long as you need it. Anything we can do to make this easier, you just have to ask. Okay?"

I could feel the lump in my throat and the tears coming again, but I managed a nod. She smiled sympathetically before rushing out to save the lasagna. I was grateful that she seemed to understand how hard this was for me.

And then it was just me standing there alone in a strange room in a strange house.

I had determined that I wouldn't cry anymore so I resisted the urge to curl up on the bed and bury my face in one of the fluffy pink pillows. There was a nice little desk in the corner. The doors to a spacious closet were slightly ajar, and Granddad had already deposited my suitcases in the corner. I could try to put some of my things away, but I wasn't anywhere near ready to accept that I would be staying.

I just stood there immobilized for about five minutes, until finally I went into the bathroom, turned on the fan, sat on the edge of the tub, and let the hot scalding tears that were burning behind my eyes come out. Better now than at dinner, I thought. Afterwards, as I washed my face, I promised myself that I would be done with crying for a good long time.

I almost broke that promise a short time later when Granddad said a very tender prayer before dinner about how thankful he was that I was there. It turned out to be a very nice meal. Myra was an amazing cook and I ate a lot, which pleased her. They kept the conversation light and upbeat. I was grateful that they were avoiding the *big kiss* topic – although I imagine they had both already seen the picture online.

I decided to ask about the little girl next door.

"Oh, that would be Abbey Roberts." Myra said with a sympathetic tone in her voice.

"And the boy is Grayson." Granddad chimed in. I blushed because he had obviously seen me looking at him.

Myra nodded and made a sort of clucking mother hen noise. "Those two have been through a lot this last year," she sighed.

Granddad explained. "They lost their mother and sister in a car wreck back in January. That ice storm I was talking about." He shook his head.

"How awful." I murmured.

"Their dad is a foreman over at Hadley. He works twelve hour shifts, six days a week, and so the kids are pretty much fending for themselves now. Myra makes sure they get a couple of good meals a week."

"That Grayson is a talented boy. An artist." Myra went on. "You should see his paintings, Danni. They are amazing."

"I've known him since he was a little boy," Granddad shook his head sadly. "He was always planning to study art in New York after he graduated, but now...I don't know."

"It's a shame," Myra sighed. "I think he'll be a senior this year, won't he?"

Granddad nodded. "You'll get to see some of his art on display at the school, Danni. He did a huge mural for the entrance hallway."

Maybe it was the heavy food or just pure exhaustion, but I felt myself starting to fade. I blinked as I tried to think of something to say. My head was spinning with thoughts that kept dancing away just as I tried to grab one. I felt so bad for Grayson and Abbey. What a horrible thing to lose a mom and sister. And then I thought about Mom and Mariela and wondered what they were doing right at this minute. It was only 5 o'clock in LA. Were they missing me at all? I wondered if Kim had been trying to call me. I thought of kissing Jack Corbin and then I wondered how it would feel to kiss Grayson Roberts. I blinked again to try and clear away the muddle and formulate a coherent sentence. I stifled a yawn instead.

Myra saved me by getting up to clear the dishes. I immediately got up to help, but she absolutely refused. "They'll be plenty of time for that later, dear. Right now you just need to go finish unpacking and get ready for bed. You are about to drop. We'll stop by later to see if you need anything."

I didn't argue. My body felt like it weighed a ton. "Thank you, Myra. The dinner was wonderful."

"I'm glad you enjoyed it. We'll have plenty of leftovers tomorrow."

"Granddad…." I faltered all of a sudden afraid that I would cry again. They were both being so kind. I walked around the table to give him a hug. "Thank you."

"You know we love you, Danni."

"Love you, too." I managed to smile at them both.

"Just give a holler if we can help with anything."

"I will. Thanks."

Back in my room with the door shut behind me, I was overwhelmed with the sense of being in a place where I didn't belong. I thought about the first time I had slept over at Kim's house and how homesick I had been even though I was having a great time. This was that feeling multiplied by a thousand. At that moment, I think I would have tried to run away if it would not have been so hurtful to Granddad. I didn't belong here. There was nothing for me here. I wanted to go home. I would get up my nerve and call Mom tomorrow. There was still time for me to be back at Commerce High with everyone else on Monday.

The shower felt good, but didn't do anything to alleviate my anxiety. At least my old, oversized sleep shirt felt familiar and safe. I pulled Macaroni out of my bag and we huddled on the strange bed together. I had never felt so alone.

The boy running in front of me was fast. I was keeping up but probably only because he was letting me.

"Slow down!" I managed to yell between gasps for breath. I could hear his laughter. I tried to remember who he was. I knew him, but I didn't.

"Think fast!" He called over his shoulder and suddenly jumped sideways and disappeared into the hedge by the road. I saw the break in the bushes and followed, jumping over the gully that separated the grass from the pavement.

I had to stop and catch my breath, bending forward and taking in huge gulps of air. When I looked up I realized that we were in someone's yard – or, to be more precise, what used to be someone's yard. The house had burned down long ago and all that was left were some blackened columns on either side of three large stone steps that seemed to lead up to nowhere. The boy was standing on the top step looking at where the house had once stood.

"Watch the first step," he called over his shoulder. "It's wobbly."

I made my way through the overgrown grass and felt the first step shift under my feet as I jumped up to stand beside him. I couldn't believe my eyes. The ground where the house had been was covered in a carpet of the most exquisite, tiny, periwinkle blue flowers. There were thousands of them and they drifted on past where the house would have been into the deserted backyard area.

"How beautiful!" I exclaimed.

The boy looked at me and smiled.

"Beauty for ashes," he said.

I woke up abruptly and it took me a minute to realize where I was. Someone had covered me with a light cotton blanket. The blinds were drawn and the overhead light had been turned off, but there was a gentle glow coming from the closet. The house was completely still.

I sat up and tried to remember the dream, but it was already slipping away. The green digital readout on the desk clock announced a new minute in time. It was 2:47 in the middle of the night, but I was wide awake. My internal clock was definitely confused.

I slipped out of bed and felt behind the blinds for the sliding door latch. Stepping out into the warm night air, I was completely unprepared for the magical scene that awaited me. The field behind the house was aglow with tiny swirling lights. There must have been thousands of fireflies flitting through the air, swirling, blinking on and off in a delightful ballet. In the distance, the massive old trees that fronted the woods sparkled like a row of cathedrals, every limb filled with dancing, twinkling little stars. For a moment, I forgot where I was and let myself be transported into their glowing, mystical kingdom.

They are weaving magic.

A crashing sound from somewhere beside the house brought me back to reality. I tiptoed to the side of the deck and saw that the garage light in the Roberts' house was on, and in the window I could just see the side of Grayson's head. He would stand still for a moment and then move out of sight only to come back into view a minute later. Even in the harsh bright garage light, he was breathtakingly handsome.

I realized that I had stopped breathing and felt silly. I really wanted to see what he was working on, so I took a step forward and walked right into a metal plant stand. It made a loud screech as it scooted across the wood. I immediately jumped back and out of sight. I was mortified. What if he had seen me? My face burned with embarrassment. I stood completely still for what seemed like an eternity and then finally leaned forward to peep around the corner of the house. To my dismay, the garage light was off. I felt like such an idiot.

I leaned back against the cool glass of the sliding doors and watched the fireflies again. They put on a spectacular show. Standing there, alone in the middle of the night, everything felt so surreal. Was this really going to be my life now? I imagined Grayson standing at his bedroom window next door – looking out at the fireflies and wondering the same thing. Malvern was a long way from LA and New York…it felt like the edge of oblivion.

CHAPTER 3

"Knock, knock." Myra poked her head into the room as I sat up and rubbed the hair out of my eyes. Bright light was filtering in from behind the drapes. I must have really overslept. She entered carrying a large mug which she deposited on the desk.

"Hey sweetie, I am so sorry to wake you. I don't know if you are a coffee drinker, but I made my own little version of a latte for you."

"What time is it?" A latte sounded good right now.

"It's 10 o'clock." She immediately waved away my gasp. "No, it's okay, dear. You needed a little extra rest. I was going to let you sleep longer, but you have a visitor."

"A visitor?" I was sitting up now and completely awake. Who would be visiting me at my Granddad's house?

"Yes, and I just couldn't tell her no. It's the little girl next door...Abbey...she's outside and wants to talk to you. Would you mind?" I smiled at the thought of the little swirling princess and then I remembered last night and her gorgeous brother in the garage. I felt my face getting red.

"Oh. Okay. Give me just a minute and I'll be there."

"Thanks, Danni. You'll see what I mean."

I jumped up and pulled on a pair of shorts and raked a comb through my hair. I thought about what had happened last night and really hoped her brother wouldn't be with her. There was no time for heroic make-up efforts. I took a few sips of Myra's latte and it was actually really good…it tasted of caramel and cream. My favorite.

Myra was waiting for me by the front door. Past her, I could see Abbey on the walkway, and she immediately brought another smile to my face. Her hair was knotted up into a bun and she was dressed in a bright pink swimsuit with matching flip flops that sported huge flowers on top. Pink polka dot water wings decorated each arm and she had topped her outfit off with an oversized pair of swim goggles that hung loosely around her neck. Her little face was scrunched up in thought under her big pink glasses.

Myra looked at me and stifled a laugh. "I tried to get her to come in, but she said she would wait for you out there." As I walked out, I was relieved that Grayson was nowhere in sight.

"Hi! Good morning. I hear you wanted to see me." I smiled and tried not to be condescending. I always hated it when bigger kids did that to me.

"Are you the princess?" Her question took me by surprise although, after I thought about it for a second it probably shouldn't have…she was definitely in the "Pink Princess" phase of life.

"No. I'm Danni." I wasn't sure what else to say. She recoiled and made a face and I tried not to laugh because her expression was hysterical.

"Danni!? That's a boy's name!" She exclaimed.

"Well, it's short for Danielle. My friends just call me Danni."

She thought about this for a minute and then gave me a huge smile. I had obviously passed her princess inspection.

"My name is Abigail Elizabeth Roberts."

"That's a really pretty name. Do your friends call you Abbey?"

"My brother does…and Pax."

"Who's Pax?"

"He's my friend."

"Oh." She really was adorable. "That's nice."

"You can call me Abbey, too."

"Well, thank you, Abbey. And I hope you'll call me Danni."

"Do you know how to swim, Danni?" I could see where this was headed and I was a little concerned about how to handle it.

"Yes, I do. It looks like you are learning. Do you like it?"

She nodded. "We are going to a swim party. Do you want to come?"

I didn't realize it, but Myra was still listening from the doorway. "Oh, Danni, that is a great idea! It's just up the street at the clubhouse. They've been doing this for several years now. On the last weekend before school starts, the kids all go swimming and the teachers prepare a big lunch in the rec hall afterward. You should go. You'll get to meet some of your classmates. It'll be fun."

My classmates. That sounded like I was in kindergarten. I wasn't sure how to say no and not disappoint Abbey. I turned to Myra.

"But I just got here..."

Myra didn't let me finish. "Oh, that's okay, dear. You'll have a great time and I'll get the grocery shopping done while you are there."

"Yay!" Abbey jumped up and down, clapping in delight. I was a little annoyed at Myra because I couldn't get out of it now.

"Grayson says we are leaving at eleven o'clock sharp!"

Grayson? I felt so stupid. Of course, Grayson would be going, too. I wanted to run back in the house and hide under the covers. What if he saw me last night, peering at him through the garage window like some stalker? How embarrassing. It was too late to think up some other excuse. Abbey was already running back over to her yard, but she called to me.

"See you at eleven, Princess Danielle!" She stopped and did a little curtsy and disappeared into the garage.

Back in the house, Myra seemed genuinely excited, and I tried not to let my irritation show.

"I know you are tired, Danni, but you'll have a great time – there's usually forty or fifty kids there. Did you pack a swimsuit?"

I nodded. I wished now that I had listened to Kim and bought that really cute two piece at the mall. My swimsuit was a lame one piece meant for swimming, not partying. Myra motioned me into the kitchen.

"You need to eat something – but something light if you are going to swim. How about a bowl of cereal? Do you like the kind with marshmallows or the healthy stuff?"

It was hard to stay angry at Myra for long.

"Marshmallows, please." We both laughed as she poured herself a bowl too.

"Where's Granddad?"

"He wanted to be here this morning, but he got called in to work. It's just for a couple of hours though."

I decided to venture into awkward territory. "Did my mom call?"

"He talked to her last night for a long time."

And…and….???? Did she say anything about me coming home? My heart was racing.

"She asked how you were doing, and she said to tell you she is overnighting the rest of your stuff. It should be here on Tuesday."

For a moment I thought I actually might faint. That was Mom's way of giving me her final answer on my exile. I wasn't going home anytime soon no matter how much I called and begged. It was true then – she really wanted me out of the house. It would finally just be her and Mariela.

I couldn't swallow another bite. Myra was still talking but I couldn't hear what she was saying. I excused myself and ran down the hall to my strange new room. I wanted to keep running but where could I go? The answer was nowhere. And Jack Corbin wasn't going to land in the field behind the house and whisk me away either. I had to deal with this.

I finally pulled myself together. I just needed time to come up with a plan. For now I had to go along with everything that was happening, and that included going to this stupid pool party. I only had a few minutes to get ready, but it didn't take that. The suit slipped on easily, and thanks to Kim, at least my cover-up was feminine and pretty. My plan was to hide behind my sunglasses and become invisible if possible.

There was a timid knock on my door. "Abbey is here, Danni. Are you ready?"

"Be right there." I took one last look in the mirror. I wasn't anything like Mariela. I had asked Mom one time if she thought I was pretty, and all she would say was that I was "pretty enough." Well, I was pretty enough for Jack Corbin to kiss me, so that was something.

I was too embarrassed to look directly at Myra as I walked out. I felt bad about how I had acted. She handed me a small tote bag.

"Oh, good. You've got sunglasses. I put a towel and some sunscreen in there for you, and one of my hats just in case the sun gets to be too much." I could tell by her subdued tone that I had hurt her feelings. I told myself it was her own fault. She was forcing me to do this.

"I hope you'll have a good time."

I took the bag with a quick "thanks" and walked out the door. Abbey was waiting. She smiled at me brightly. She had added a pair of star shaped sunglasses over her glasses. Her little frame was completely overwhelmed by her swim ensemble, but she was so eager it was impossible not to smile back.

"See!" She called to her brother, who was standing at the edge of their driveway watching us. "I told you she would come!" Abbey grabbed my hand and pulled me toward him.

Grayson was wearing brown, baggy shorts, a white t-shirt, and oddly enough some sort of loose, unbuckled ankle boot with no socks. It was an easy going, artsy look. With his tall frame, dark hair, and sunglasses, he could have passed for a model or rock star on the cover of a magazine. Even the beach tote slung casually over his shoulder couldn't lessen the appeal. I could feel him sizing me up from behind his shades. Normally I would have looked away, but today I was filled with so much of my own despair that I didn't even care.

"This is Danielle." Abby announced as we got closer.

"Hi." He nodded.

"Hi." I wasn't sure what to say – and it was obvious that he wasn't going to initiate the conversation. I would have to go first. "I hope this is okay. Abbey invited me."

"Yeah, sure."

"Let's go!" Abbey was tugging Grayson's hand now. "We have to get Tyler." She let go of his hand and ran on ahead. We followed in silence. The street was quiet and deserted. I tried to think of something to say as we headed up the hill. I remembered Granddad saying that the clubhouse was on the next street over so maybe the awkward silence wouldn't last too long.

At least Abbey was a talker. She suddenly turned around and looked at me.

"He's really glad you are here."

"Abbey." Grayson's tone was cautionary. Did she mean Grayson?

"Who?" I asked before I could stop myself.

"Pax!" She exclaimed excitedly. "He's been waiting for you!"

"Abbey, that's enough." Grayson's tone was stern.

It was already a hot day, but I felt a cold chill run through my body as goose bumps popped up on my arms and neck. Something wasn't quite right.

Grayson obviously felt the need to explain. "She's got an imaginary friend."

"Oh." I nodded, still feeling like someone had walked over my grave.

"He's not imaginary," Abbey circled back and took my hand again. "His name is Pax and he says you are a princess!" I could sense Grayson's body tense. Without even looking, I knew that the worried frown had settled on his forehead again.

Abbey turned to her brother and put on her most irresistible face. "Can I get Tyler? Please?"

"Sure." Grayson's voice was tinged with exhaustion. Abbey took off running up the hill ahead of us, which was hard in her flip flops. At the next house she ran up the walkway and rang the doorbell. Grayson and I waited in the road. After living in LA, it was downright eerie that not a single car had passed us.

I decided to make another attempt at conversation. "My granddad tells me you are an artist." I immediately wished that I hadn't said it. It was an awkward statement that led to nowhere and let him know that we had been talking about him. I felt my cheeks flame.

He was silent for a moment, and then finally said, "I like to draw." I was trying to think of a logical question to follow up with when he surprised me by asking, "What do you like to do?"

I don't think anyone my age had ever asked me that and I had absolutely no answer. Thankfully I didn't have to come up with one because the door to the house opened and a young man came out. He immediately picked Abbey up and whirled her around as she squealed with delight, and then he came toward us carrying her like a sack of potatoes as she giggled. He had a great smile, and was dressed comfortably in swim trunks and a sleeveless t-shirt that really featured his well-defined muscles and rich tan. His hair was buzzed in a military cut.

"Hi!" He smiled and extended his hand after depositing Abbey safely to the ground.

"Hi." I was a little surprised, but I shook his hand. His grip was solid.

"I'm Tyler and you must be Danielle. Abbey has told me all about you – the new princess on Windswept." He laughed and I smiled but, as usual, I wasn't sure how to respond.

"Hey, Gray." Tyler nodded at Grayson and walked past me. In a low tone he asked, "Listen, can I hang out with you guys tonight?"

Grayson nodded. "Yeah, anytime. You know that."

"Thanks, man."

"Let's go!" Abbey demanded, pulling at Tyler's hand. "They are going to start without us!"

"Okay Sparkle Butt." Tyler good-naturedly

allowed himself to be pulled along by Abbey as we headed up the remainder of the hill.

"So, Danielle. Where are you from?" Tyler seemed very comfortable spearheading the conversation.

"Los Angeles."

He whistled. "LA. Wow. You are a long way from home." His words felt like a knife in my heart, but I tried to smile. He seemed genuinely nice.

"So how did you wind up in Malvern?"

I had no idea how to answer that. I still had Grayson's "what do you like to do" question nagging at me.

"I'm going to be staying with my grandparents for a while." I finally managed. It was all I could think to say. I should have rehearsed how I was going to handle the inevitable questions about how I got here. I wondered how long it would be before someone discovered the picture of me and *the kiss*.

"So you are going to go to school here?" He seemed surprised but pleased.

"Yes. I guess it starts Monday, right?" I realized that I had been so sure that I was going home that I hadn't even bothered to ask.

"Tuesday. Monday's a teacher work day. Then it's half a day on Tuesday and then regular time after that. Our first game is Friday night. You should come."

I nodded. "I'll try." I lied. "Do you play?"

"Yeah. It's my first year on Varsity. What do you like to do?"

There was that question again. But it made sense. Grayson was an artist, Tyler was obviously an athlete. Kim was into fashion design. Jack Corbin was an avid surfer. The question made me realize how completely unremarkable I was. What *did* I like to do? Responding that I was the invisible younger sister of Mariela Patterson probably wasn't a good idea.

Abbey saved me.

"I told you she is a princess," she said in an exasperated grown up tone that made us all laugh. "Now come on."

We could already hear loud voices and splashing up ahead. The pool turned out to be very large and nicely laid out with a kiddie pool on one end and lots of tables and lounge chairs all around. It was flanked by a modern clubhouse with big windows that overlooked the pool area. Most of the teenagers were hanging out together on the far side of the pool near the lifeguard stand. The grade-schoolers were already swimming and playing a game of toss with a huge beach ball.

I suddenly felt unsure of what to do. Grayson dropped his tote on a chair near the kiddie pool and Abbey made a bee-line into the shallow water with some other kids her age. I put my stuff down in the chair next to Grayson, hoping I wasn't being presumptuous. Tyler peeled off his t-shirt and I quickly looked away because he was in great shape and I didn't want to be caught staring. I wasn't quite ready to take off my cover up, so I found some lotion to put on – starting with my legs.

I noticed a tall, gorgeous girl leaving the group on the far side of the pool and coming our way. She was perfectly tanned and wore a tiny bikini. I was amazed to see that she was wearing some kind of wedged high heels – Kim would know what they were called – and was actually able to glide across the slippery tiles without so much as even glancing down. She made me think of a brunette version of Mariela, complete with perfect waterproof makeup and stiff hair.

She was walking right toward Grayson. He hadn't noticed and was kicking off his boots when she approached him from behind and wrapped her arms around his chest.

"Hi Gray." She said in a purring kitten voice.

"Hey!" He grabbed her hand as she walked around to face him. As she did, she looked at me with a cool lethal stare, then she completely dismissed me and positioned herself in front of Grayson.

"Aren't you going to come sit with us?" She whined.

Tyler was just finishing up his sunscreen and he obviously knew the girl.

"Go ahead, Gray. I'll watch Abbey."

Grayson nodded and followed the girl back to the group on the other side of the pool.

I felt like a complete idiot. Of course he would have a girlfriend, and of course she would look like that. She had taken one look at me and realized that I wasn't any kind of threat to her. He didn't have any obligation to sit with me, and he hadn't even bothered to introduce us.

This was the Mariela Syndrome all over again. Looking at all the popular kids grouped up on the other side of the pool, I realized that I was in a small town version of the same old high school drama show that went on at Commerce. I just hadn't expected the tortured artist type to be one of "them." Come to think of it, I was surprised that Tyler wasn't over there, too, but he didn't seem interested. He was already in the pool trying to coax Abbey out of the shallow water.

The water did look inviting, and there were two roped off lanes for serious swimmers. I slipped out of my cover up, finished with sunscreen, and tried to pretend that there weren't at least two dozen eyes watching me as I walked to the deep end and dove in. The water was colder than I had expected but I adjusted quickly. When your dad is a Navy SEAL you pretty much learn to swim before you learn to walk. Dad had always encouraged me to be physically strong. I could remember putting books into my flower covered backpack and jogging alongside him while he trained with fifty pounds of gear on his back.

Mariela went to ballet class, and I went to karate lessons. I used to be a little jealous of her pink tutus and satin slippers, but I loved pleasing my dad so I tried hard to excel at everything he challenged me with. Even our playtime had a purpose. He taught me to block and dodge and parry with a little plastic sword in our Pirates Only playhouse that I helped him build. I learned to climb walls and jump and tumble when we had to outrun a group of pretend T-Rexes on our very own castaway island. Mariela had always watched us from a distance, refusing to join in…calling me a tomboy, and I guess in a way Dad had treated me like a boy – but I didn't care. Those were the happiest times of my life.

When Dad died, it all ended, and since then I had devoted my time to becoming invisible. That's why Grayson's question had bothered me so much. I had no idea who I was now, and my cloak of invisibility had been ripped away when I stepped off the plane in Atlanta.

I sliced the water like a pro, but my heart was so heavy it felt like a rock in my chest. I stopped swimming and allowed myself to sink to the bottom of the pool.

I miss you, Dad.

I rested there until my lungs were begging for air. I kicked off and popped out of the water to find a woman watching me from the side. I immediately made her for one of the teachers who were hosting the party. I was only down for a minute – surely I wasn't in trouble. She leaned over to talk to me and I shielded my eyes from the sun to see her better.

"Was Dan Taylor your dad?"

Her question totally surprised me.

"Yes." I answered hesitantly not knowing what this was about.

She smiled. "I'm Emma Morgan. Your dad and I were…" she hesitated and seemed to be searching for the right words, "…we were friends in high school."

"Oh." I really didn't know what to say.

"I heard you were here, and I just didn't want to miss the opportunity to meet you. Your dad was…well, he was one of the good guys."

"Thank you." I felt like I should say something else but, as usual, I was at a loss for what that might be. I'd never heard of this woman before.

"Well, I'd better get back in there," she motioned towards the clubhouse. "It's really nice to meet you ….Danielle, isn't it?"

I nodded. "It's nice to meet you, too."

She gave me a big smile and then hurried away. I found the ladder and pulled myself out of the pool. I silently thanked Myra for the towel and dried off as quickly as I could and pulled on the cover up.

"Danielle! Look!" Abbey yelled at me to watch as she made a valiant effort to kick across the shallow end, water flying everywhere. "That's great, Abbey!" I smiled and waved, remembering how those first swimming victories felt. Tyler was still patiently instructing her. He seemed more like her older brother than Grayson, who was still at the table across the pool with the popular kids. I noticed that a phone was being passed around and some of them laughed and looked my way. I felt my face burn from more than the sun. I couldn't be sure, but my guess was that someone had found my infamous internet kiss and they were all having a good laugh on me.

All of a sudden I didn't care. I just wanted to go home, and if my granddad's house was home now, then that was where I was going. I tried to be nonchalant as I slipped on my shoes, grabbed the tote, and headed for the gate. I was afraid Abbey would notice and yell for me, but once I got out to the walkway, I felt like I was home free because a tall hedge blocked the view of the pool. I breathed a sigh of relief.

"Danielle?"

I had almost made it to the road when I heard someone call my name. I turned to find that Grayson had followed me out. His supermodel girlfriend was nowhere in sight. I felt my heart do an extra beat at the sight of him. He had taken off his sunglasses and those piercing, dark eyes seemed to be searching my soul.

I reprimanded myself quickly for being so stupid. He had no interest in me.

"They'll be serving lunch in a little while if you want to stay."

Did he really want me to stay? No, of course not. He was probably just thinking that Abbey would be disappointed.

"Oh, yeah, thanks. It's just that I really need to get back. I haven't even unpacked yet. I'll…I'll talk to you guys later." I waved and then turned as confidently as I could and made my way down the street. I didn't look back until I reached the main road, and when I did, he was gone. I practically ran across the street and down the hill to Granddad's house.

CHAPTER 4

I had never felt so out of place and alone. All I wanted to do was crawl back under Myra's fluffy comforter and sleep for days, but to my dismay, I realized that Myra's car was gone. She must really have gone grocery shopping and Granddad hadn't returned from work yet. I was on my own.

I plopped my tote down on the stoop and started searching around the door and in the plant urns to see if a spare key might be hidden anywhere. I came up empty and decided to go around the house to the back deck...maybe I'd have better luck there.

As I rounded the corner of the house, I noticed that the garage door of Grayson and Abbey's house was wide open. I immediately thought of seeing Grayson through the garage window last night. He had been so intent on whatever he was working on. It had to be a painting. I was curious...I really wanted to see it.

I glanced up the street. Still not a soul or a car in sight. I stepped over the mulched flower bed that separated the yards and walked up the drive into the coolness at the edge of the garage. It took a minute for my eyes to adjust, but it was obvious that the garage had been split in half – one side left neat and open for a car; the other had been turned into an art studio. There was an easel and a table littered with pots of paint and brushes and boxes of colored chalks and pencils. A faint smell of oils and turpentine floated on the air. The canvas Grayson had been working on was facing toward the window. I would have to walk all the way into the garage if I wanted to see it.

I hesitated for a minute and listened. Everything was quiet. I got up my nerve and walked on into the garage. I actually gasped audibly when I saw the painting. A cool rush of wind filled the garage at the same time, causing papers on the table to rustle and giving me goose bumps for the second time today.

The painting wasn't at all what I expected, but I could immediately see why Granddad said Grayson was so talented. It was exquisite in every way. The central figure was a young woman. She was more beautiful than anyone I had ever seen. Her face was incredibly noble and her soft blue eyes were filled with strength and courage. She had long blonde hair that was tangled and dirty, and on top of her head was an unusual crown that swept back from a large gemstone in the center of her forehead. Her clothes were soiled and in tatters, but it was obvious that it had once been the clothing of royalty. She was huddled against a stone wall in a tower room. Behind her was a large open window that revealed a view from on high. The landscape below was alien, barren, and bleak with only a strange rock formation in the distance for a view. She was obviously a prisoner because there was a large metal clasp around her reddened ankle that was secured to a chain on the wall. The painting was so realistic that for a moment I felt like I was standing in the room with her – that I could reach out and take her hand. I realized that I had been holding my breath as I studied it.

Another heavy gust of wind sent the papers around me flying and brought me back to reality. I was trespassing into Grayson's private world, but it was mesmerizing. I felt like I had walked into a story and I wanted to know more. I took one last look at the beautiful princess and quickly left the garage. Jumping back over the flowers, I headed to the back of Granddad's house. A breeze had definitely picked up and the sky was clouding over.

I climbed the steps to the deck outside my room and searched for a key on the ledge above the sliding door, under the mat, and under the plant stand that had given away my presence last night. Nothing. I trekked to the far side of the house but didn't have any better luck at the kitchen door. I would have to wait until someone came home. I circled back around and sat down on the top step of the deck and leaned against the railing. The shadows on the field danced as the sun slid in and out of the clouds. The breeze felt nice. Across the field, the giant oaks that fronted the woods looked like tall sentries guarding whatever secrets the forest held.

I suddenly yawned, feeling very tired. I must have drifted off to sleep for just a second because I imagined that the field had morphed into a sea of mist, and the woods appeared more like a distant country – another land. Someone was walking through the swirling mist. He turned to me and waved.

"What are you doing out here, young'un?" My head jerked up as Granddad's voice snapped me out of the dream. He was standing at the foot of the steps holding my abandoned tote bag.

"Hey Granddad. I'm locked out." I smiled.

"I can see that." He had a worried look on his face. "Myra said you were going to the swim party."

"Well, I did." He could see that I had been swimming. "I just didn't want to stay for the whole thing."

"Mm." He wasn't exactly cross, but he did look concerned. "Well, it's a good thing I stopped and got this made." He held up a house key attached to a ridiculously oversized hubcap keychain. He broke into a smile and winked. "Now you've got your own key to the front door and you're not apt to lose it as long as it's attached to this thing. Let's go around and see if it works."

It did, and it felt good to be inside again. Even if Granddad's house didn't feel like home yet, it still felt safe.

"Thanks, Granddad."

"I've got something else for you, too." He reached in his pocket and pulled out a phone. "It's activated and ready to use. I've already programmed our numbers in there. So no more getting stranded outside." He frowned again and his voice sounded stern with concern. "You call us."

"I will, Granddad." I hugged him. "I'm sorry. I was fine though. Really. Wow. This is nice." It was just like Kim's.

"Let me know if you need any help using it." He lightened up a little and laughed. "Although I'm guessing you could show me a thing or two."

We both laughed.

"You know," Granddad winked at me, "I think I could go for a slice of Myra's lasagna right about now. What about you?"

"No, thanks. I'm okay." I shook my head as Granddad scooped out a huge slice of lasagna and put it in the microwave. Seeming to ignore my answer, he got two plates and two forks out of the drawer. I gave up and plopped down on a stool at the kitchen counter.

"So what happened at the pool?"

"It was nice," I tried to sound upbeat. "The pool is really great." At least that was the truth.

He nodded. "They did a good job with it. So, did you meet anyone interesting?" He pulled the lasagna out and cut off a big slice and handed me a plate. It did smell good.

"I met Tyler."

"He's a good kid." Granddad came around to join me at the counter and we talked in between bites. "He's got a good head on his shoulders. He's going to need it with that crazy family of his."

"What do you mean?" I found that I was definitely curious about Tyler.

Granddad shook his head. "His dad left a few months ago. Moved back to Atlanta. He's been running around. Drinking. Up until last year they could have been parents of the year. I don't know what gets into people."

"He seems to get along well with Grayson and Abbey."

"Well, that's because Tyler was dating their sister."

"The one in the car wreck?"

Granddad nodded. "They had been sweethearts since grade school. Pretty much inseparable."

That explained a lot. Tyler had been a part of Grayson and Abbey's family for a long time. And that's why none of the girls were hanging on him at the pool even though he was about as all-American good-looking as it gets. He was still off limits.

Granddad polished off the last of his lasagna and leaned back on the stool. "Tyler reminds me a lot of your dad at that age. Did he tell you he's the starting quarterback for the Mavericks this year?"

"He told me he was on the team." The mention of Dad made me think of the teacher. "Oh, and I met Emma Morgan. She said she was a friend of Dad's."

"Mm." Granddad nodded. "Now Emma was your Dad's girlfriend for a little while."

"Really?" I realized I didn't know anything about my dad when he was young.

"Oh, yeah." Granddad got up and went to a drawer in the coffee table and brought back a photo album. He flipped through and found a prom picture of Emma and Dad. Dad was handsome even as a teenager, although his taste in tuxedos left a lot to be desired. They looked like a cute "most-likely-to-get-married" type of couple. It was odd to think that she could have been my mother.

"She had her cap set on him for the longest," Granddad continued.

"What happened?"

"Well, your dad always had very definite ideas about what he wanted to do in life. He had a sense of purpose from a very early age. His dream was to serve in the Navy. He was always working toward that goal. Always pushing himself to be the very best he could be at everything. Emma had her own plans, too, and they couldn't quite get them to mesh. They tried for a while after high school, but wound up going their separate ways in college. It happens when you are young."

We browsed through more photos in the album with Granddad pointing out Dad's friends and filling in the details. It was interesting to see Dad as a young man. The last picture in the album was Mom and Dad's wedding photo. I had seen that one before, but not in a long time.

"And Mom?" I had to ask. "Did she fit into Dad's plans?"

Granddad sighed, closed the album, and took it back to its drawer. I could tell the pictures and the question had made him sad. He was thoughtful for a moment.

"Your mom is a beautiful woman." His statement completely shocked me. I had never thought of Mom as being beautiful – she was just…Mom.

"Your dad was smitten from the moment he met her." Granddad picked up our plates and carried them around to the sink. "You look a lot like her, you know." I was stunned. I felt like running over to the hall mirror to see if I had changed since this morning.

I shook my head. "Mariela is the pretty one." It was a fact that I had always known and made peace with.

Granddad laughed and then checked himself. "Well, there's a difference between beauty from a bottle and natural beauty." He smiled and winked at me. "And let's not forget you get some of those good looks from your old granddad!"

I tried to smile. All of this had taken me by surprise. Granddad had me mixed up with someone else, and surely there was more to my parent's love story than just physical attraction. Granddad must have read my mind.

"It wasn't just that she was pretty. Your mom had all those qualities Dan admired. She was strong and smart and independent – a single mom putting herself through school, determined to make a better life for her daughter. Your dad wanted to help. They were really happy for a while. They had big plans."

"What happened?" I felt the words catch in my throat.

"I don't know young'un," Granddad shook his head and sighed again, patting me on the back as he came around the counter. "The military life isn't easy. Too much time apart, maybe." He was thoughtful for a moment. "But I know one thing, Danni, he was crazy about you. He told me once that you were the best thing that had ever happened in his life. He cherished every minute he got to spend with you."

I nodded, too choked up to respond, as we heard Myra's car pull into the driveway. I was glad for the interruption. The day had been far too full of emotional ups and downs. Granddad seemed relieved, too.

"That'll be my girl with a ton of groceries!" he laughed. "Tell you what. I'll go help her get them in and you go get that chlorine out of your hair so she doesn't fuss at us both."

I slipped off the stool and gave him a hug. "Thanks, Granddad."

"Love you, young'un." We both sounded like we were struggling to control our emotions, but he managed a chuckle as he walked towards the front door. "And if she asks about the lasagna, I'm going to tell her you ate it all!"

"Granddad!" I scolded and he laughed as he disappeared out the door. I watched him through the front window as he helped Myra out of the car and gave her a kiss. They seemed so happy. I blinked and felt my nose sting with unshed tears. I tried to imagine my dad feeling that way about Mom. He must have at one time. I wondered if I would ever feel that way about someone.

As I headed to the shower, Grayson's question echoed in my mind. Everyone seemed to know their purpose in the world except me.

After the shower, I wiped the steam off the mirror and stared at my reflection for a long time, trying to see the resemblance to my mom. Mom was always raving about how gorgeous Mariela was. I had always thought of myself as petite and plain compared to Mariela's towering blonde brilliance. Was it possible that I was pretty too? Could it even be possible that Mom had exiled me to Granddad's house because she was afraid I might make the same kind of mistakes she had made when she was young?

Nothing made any sense anymore.

I really wanted to talk to Kim, but deep down I was horribly embarrassed by everything that had happened. Kim's family was normal and wonderful. Both her parents were kind and supportive. They would never have sent her away for kissing a boy. I had spent a lot of time at their house my freshman year and they had always treated me like one of their own, which made me feel wonderful and sad all at the same time. When Kim was at my house it was a different story. Mom barely acknowledged us. Kim was such a good friend that she never said anything, but I was sure she wondered about it. And now this. I just wasn't ready to talk about any of it yet. I would call her later.

I rummaged through my luggage to find something comfortable to wear and decided that it was time to unpack before my clothes became impossibly wrinkled. I was thousands of miles away from everything that made me feel like me – seeing a few familiar items couldn't hurt. Besides, there was no point in postponing the inevitable. An hour later when Myra poked her head in the door, everything was neatly put away and the luggage stowed in the corner of the closet. She didn't say anything, but I could tell she was pleased.

"Sweetie, your Granddad was wondering if you'd like to take a ride into Hadley with us. He's been looking for a laptop for you – you'll need one for school – and he says he's found a good deal. We can grab some dinner while we are out."

"That sounds nice."

"The computer store closes at five so we'll need to leave pretty soon."

"I'll just be a minute." If we were going to eat out, I should at least try to look presentable. I quickly changed into one of the outfits that Kim and I bought, smoothed my hair, added a hint of blush and mascara, and topped it off with tinted lip gloss and some drop earrings. I had to at least make an effort for Granddad.

I could see the approval on Myra's face when I emerged from my room. As we headed toward the car, I couldn't help glancing over at the Roberts' house. There was no sign of Grayson or Abbey, but I did notice the garage door was closed now, so someone must be there. I wondered what their dad was like and if Tyler had come home with them. I felt bad that I had probably alienated the only people who were apt to be my friends here.

The rest of the evening was as pleasant as could be expected. Hadley turned out to be much larger than Malvern and we stopped off at Hadley Aerospace on the way, which was like a large futuristic city all by itself. I was quite surprised. Since we didn't have special clearance, we were only allowed in the lobby, but even the lobby was like a theme park attraction. Granddad seemed so proud to introduce me to the security guard at the desk.

"What do you do there, Granddad?" I asked as we made our way back to the car.

"That's classified. If I told you, I'd have to kill you." Granddad winked and laughed.

Myra rolled her eyes. "If I had a dollar for every time I've heard that one!"

We made it to the computer shop just before it closed, and then headed to High Grove Café for dinner, which turned out to be a trendy downtown watering hole. It didn't strike me as the kind of place Granddad and Myra would choose to eat at, but there were lots of young people there and I suspected they were trying to show me that I hadn't completely fallen off the face of the earth.

I kept yawning on the ride home. It seemed to be getting dark early because it had started to rain and the sound of the windshield wipers was lulling me to sleep. Like an old lady, I was ready for bed at eight o'clock. Pretty sad, I thought, but the jet lag and traumatic events of the past two days had really caught up with me. I was actually glad when we turned onto Windswept and headed down the hill to Granddad's. I noticed the lights were on in Grayson's house. I couldn't explain it, but I felt relieved to know that he and Abbey and Tyler were next door. In the brief time I had spent with them today, there had been some unspoken connection. Maybe it was just that we shared the common bond of family dysfunction. Whatever it was, I felt bad for bailing on the swim party and I wanted to salvage the friendships if possible.

But that would have to wait until tomorrow. I could barely keep my eyes open. I said goodnight to Granddad and Myra and went to my room. I remembered that I was supposed to call Kim but I was too tired. I pulled on some pajama shorts and a matching t-shirt and brushed my teeth. Once in bed, I reached for Macaroni, and like so many other nights, I unzipped the secret pouch, pulled out the key, and slipped it around my neck.

CHAPTER 5

I don't know what woke me up. A rumble of thunder maybe. But whatever it was, I was wide awake.

The house was very still and my room was dark. I could hear the rain pattering onto the deck. I glanced over at the clock, surprised that I had slept through most of the night. It was 4:17 – too early to get up but too late to try and go back to sleep.

And then I heard it. A tinkling sound almost like laughter. I pushed back the drapes just in time to see the field behind the house illuminated by some distant lightning. I could have sworn I saw someone out there. I strained to see anything, but it was very dark and the rain-drenched window wasn't helping. I slipped the latch on the door and slid it open just a crack. There it was again. Talking and laughter. I froze and felt my hair stand on end for the third time. That was Abbey's voice. What could she be doing out in the field in the dark?

I quickly slipped on my sneakers, and grabbed a hoodie and a flashlight that I had seen earlier on the top shelf of the closet. Out on the deck, I shined the light into the field. It took me a minute to locate her because she was almost to the woods, but I was sure it was Abbey – a little figure dressed in pink. I could just make out that she had a backpack on.

I was down the stairs and over to Grayson's back door in moments. I pounded and yelled his name just as lightning filled the sky again. The thunder came not far behind it. The storm was getting closer. I couldn't wait for Grayson, I had to go get her now.

The weeds were high and slashed at my bare legs. I was soaked before I got halfway to her. Her little figure kept bouncing in and out of the flashlight's beam. I glanced back over my shoulder and was relieved to see that there were now upstairs and downstairs lights on in Grayson's house. As I got closer to Abbey I could hear her talking. She was having a conversation with the thin air next to her. I wondered if she might be sleepwalking. I had read somewhere that waking a sleepwalker too quickly could be dangerous. I would need to be very careful not to startle her.

Another wave of spidery lightning darted across the sky, providing an eerie backdrop for the towering trees up ahead. The thunder followed immediately. I knew that if Abbey woke up now she was going to be severely traumatized. I glanced back toward the houses and could see two people running my way. It had to be Grayson and Tyler.

I slowed down and matched Abbey's pace, staying just a few steps behind her.

"Hi Abbey. It's Danni." She didn't acknowledge me at all. She kept walking, but she had stopped talking.

I edged a little closer. "It's time to go back to bed now, sweetie."

She stopped.

"Abbey?" I asked gently. "Everything is okay. Grayson is coming." I had the feeling that she was waking up. I could hear Grayson rushing through the weeds toward us. Before I could turn to warn him not to scare her, the sky lit up again. This time the thunder was deafening and it shook the ground like an earthquake. Abbey let out a terrified scream just as Grayson rushed by me and picked her up. Tyler was only a few yards behind, but before he reached us, I felt something sting my head and then my arms. Suddenly we were being pelted with ice balls.

"It's hail!" Tyler yelled. "Get under the trees." The forest was a lot closer than the houses behind us so it made sense to take cover there. I tried to shine the flashlight to show the way, but all it revealed was that the hail was getting larger. It packed a serious sting. I could hear Abbey crying even though Grayson was trying to run and shield her at the same time.

A horrible growling noise caused me to glance over my shoulder. I stopped in sheer terror. It was like something out of a movie, only infinitely more terrifying…a funnel cloud lit from within by a strange glow. It descended slowly to the ground and immediately started hurling debris.

"Tornado!" I managed to scream out the warning even though it felt like my breath was being pulled right out of me. Tyler whirled around and yanked me forward as he yelled to Grayson.

"Look for the rock! Get to the swimming hole!" He grabbed the flashlight from me and scanned the tree line as we ran toward it.

"There!" He yelled as the beam caught a huge boulder sticking out of the ground. Grayson was running ahead with Abbey and Tyler and I were right behind them. I didn't dare look back at the monster that was gaining on us.

The limbs on the massive oaks were thrashing wildly as we ran past the huge rock and underneath the trees, but at least their coverage softened the sting of the hail. Tyler ran ahead with the flashlight, showing us the way.

"Here!" Tyler shouted to me above the roar. "It used to be an old swimming hole. We need to get as low as we can!" He tossed the flashlight down the bank, and it lit up a muddy gully littered with empty soda bottles. He quickly grabbed a large thick vine that was hanging from one of the trees and lowered himself down.

"It's okay, Abbey. Tyler is going to catch you." Grayson was already on his belly handing Abbey down the bank to Tyler.

"Got her!" Tyler yelled, and then Grayson let go of her hands. There was such a sense of trust between the three of them. The wind was whipping my hair in front of my face, making it hard to see in the dim light, but it looked as if Grayson was going to try and help me down. Instead, I quickly grabbed the vine and slid down the muddy embankment, silently thanking Dad for all those wall-climbing trips to the mall. Grayson was right behind me.

"Quick! Get on the ground!" Tyler was yelling. It sounded like a freight train was bearing down on us. Abbey had stopped crying and had wrapped herself around my legs. I pulled her down on the ground next me and held her as tight as I could, covering her head with my hoodie. I felt Grayson lie down almost on top of us. Tyler got down on the other side of Abbey and reached across to link arms with Grayson. They were trying to offer as much protection to us as they could.

I had been through several earthquakes, but never a tornado, and this one, with its interior cylinder of light, didn't look like any that I had ever seen on television. The flashlight was eerily tumbling around on its own adding to the chaos around us. We appeared to lying in an old creek bed, but it was hard to see anything since one side of my face was in the mud and my eyes were full of water. I held on to Abbey as tightly as I could.

Everything felt so surreal, as if time itself were slowing down around us. How could this be happening? Three days ago, I was in Westridge Mall in LA getting my first kiss from Jack Corbin. Now I was lying in a trench in the mud in the middle of a tornado with three people that I barely knew. I could feel Grayson's body pressed against me and his breath on my neck.

"It's going to be okay," I thought I heard him whisper, but I couldn't be sure. The roar around us was deafening and the branches overhead sounded like they were in a battle to the death with the sky. It didn't feel okay, but his words were comforting just the same.

I closed my eyes and concentrated on Grayson's strong arm over me. Something stabbed my leg, but I still kept my eyes closed. The winds had begun to sound like screaming women and just when I thought I couldn't stand it any longer, it all stopped. The rain became just a drizzle, the howling stopped, and everything went quiet. I finally opened my eyes and to my surprise there was an early morning sky peeking through the tree branches overhead. Their limbs were still intact, creating dark silhouettes against the impending dawn. I actually heard a bird chirp somewhere not too far away.

"Is everyone okay?" Grayson jumped up. "Abbey?!" Abbey wriggled out from under me and adjusted her glasses.

"I'm okay."

Grayson picked her up. "You sure?"

She nodded.

Tyler extended a hand to help me up and I winced as I put weight on my leg. I felt a little trickle of blood run down my leg. I was just about to bend over and look at it more closely when the full impact of what had happened hit me. I tried to speak, but could barely make the sound.

"Granddad!" I finally managed a panicked shriek. Before anyone could stop me, I grabbed the vine and scrambled up the embankment.

"Danni, wait!" Tyler yelled, but I was already at the top. I had to make sure that Granddad and Myra were okay. I could hear someone climbing up behind me, but I didn't wait. There was enough early morning light to make out the short path under the trees back to the field without the flashlight.

I burst into the clearing, but stopped immediately. I was paralyzed by a wave of horror. I couldn't make out even one house across the field. The sky was growing lighter by the second as morning approached, but I couldn't make out anything – not even debris. I regained my ability to move, and started to run again, but Tyler had caught up with me and put a steel grip on my arm.

"Danni, no! It's not safe!" I tried to get free, but he refused to let me go. It wasn't that the houses had been damaged, it was as if the houses had never been there

– there was no sign of them at all; as far as I could tell the field simply gave way to a hill covered with brush.

It occurred to me that I must have gotten turned around. I needed to go back down in the gully and up the other side. I whirled around and tried to get past Tyler, who was still gripping my arm.

"I got confused – it's on the other side."

Tyler refused to let go of me even though I tried to wrench free.

"No, it's not, Danni."

"Yes it is. You can see that there aren't any houses on this side." I felt stupid for stating the obvious, but Tyler tightened his grip and pointed to the big boulder that we had just passed.

"See, there's the rock where we went in. We're in the right place."

I felt a little hysterical. All I could think about was Granddad and Myra. I was grasping at straws.

"That's not the same rock. I'm sure there are lots of big rocks like that around here."

"It's the same rock, Danni. Trust me."

"You don't know that, Tyler. Please let me go. I have to find Granddad and Myra."

"I do know, Danni. Look." He pulled me toward the rock and pointed the flashlight to some writing on the side. I could see a heart carved into the stone, and in the center were the words 'Terry + Tyler 4 ever.'

"I put that there." He said firmly. "We're in the right place." He finally let go of my arm.

Grayson and Abbey emerged from the trees behind us.

"Where's our house, Grayson?" Abbey sounded scared. For a moment we all just stood there in stunned silence, looking across the field, waiting for the sun to come out and prove us wrong.

"I don't know, Abbey. We have to find it. Let's just wait till it gets a little lighter, okay?" Grayson was still holding her and he smoothed her hair and kissed the top of her head. She nodded.

"I'm sorry," I said feebly. I felt like I should apologize. A four year old seemed to be handling this better than me. I was cold and wet and starting to shake, and I could still feel blood running down my leg into my shoe.

"Here," Tyler took my elbow gently this time. "Let's take a look at your leg." He helped me onto the rock. There was a nice little flat spot where I imagine many teenage couples had sat before me. Even though the sky was much lighter now, Tyler still used the flashlight to examine my leg.

"Mmm. You've got a good-sized piece of a twig in there. This might hurt." He pulled it out quickly and I flinched as more warm blood oozed out and ran down my leg. Without missing a beat, he reached down and ripped off the bottom of his t-shirt and quickly wrapped it around my calf.

"There, that should help with the bleeding, but you're probably going to need some stitches."

"Thanks." I said again weakly. I felt like a complete idiot. Tyler was the one who had been the nicest to me and I had totally yelled at him.

"I'm sorry." I said again as he finished tying off the bandage. He looked up and gave me an earnest nod.

"It's okay, Danni. We just have to figure out what has happened. But it's going to be okay."

I nodded. I could see why Granddad said Tyler reminded him of Dad. He was good and brave and strong and kept his head under pressure.

"That was some nice work getting up the bank back there." He smiled. I knew his compliment was an attempt to lighten things up.

"Thanks." I was pleased that he had noticed.

Through all of this, Grayson had been staring across the field. The sun was actually peeping over the horizon now and it was apparent that the houses of Windswept were nowhere to be seen. Grayson carried Abbey over and sat her down next to me on the rock.

"Abbey, I need for you to do me a favor." Grayson looked at me pointedly over Abbey's head, his eyes pleading for my help.

"Okay." Abbey was curious.

"Tyler and I need to walk across the field and see what happened to the houses. I need for you to stay here and take care of Danielle."

"No." Abbey whined. "I want to go with you." It was clear that she was afraid and wanted her big brother – not me.

"I know." Grayson said gently. "But Danni's leg is hurt and she can't walk. We can't leave her here alone, can we? She needs you to take care of her."

Abbey was having a hard time coming up with a reply. As I looked at the two of them so close together, I realized that Abbey was going to grow up to be as beautiful as her brother was handsome. Her pink glasses did a good job of hiding what a pretty little girl she was.

"But…" she was trying to think of an excuse to go with them.

"And Abbey, I promise that we won't ever go out of your sight, okay? You'll be able to see us at all times. Can you do this for me? Can you stay here with Danni?" His gorgeous eyes met mine again and they spoke volumes. He was trying to protect his little sister from whatever might be across the field.

"Okay." Abbey relented.

"That's my girl." Grayson kissed her on the forehead. "Now you take care of Danielle, and we'll be back in just a few minutes."

Grayson looked at me pointedly as if to say "please take care of my sister." I nodded my understanding. Tyler was waiting at his side as if the two of them had already discussed this. They didn't hesitate, but immediately sprinted off across the field.

Abbey sighed. "I guess it's just you and me, kid," she said in such a grown-up tone that I had to laugh. I hugged her and she wrapped her arms around my waist as we watched the guys move further and further away. When they were almost across the field, Grayson turned and waved and Abbey waved back.

The morning sun was fully up and even the first rays felt warm. I could feel the mud drying on my face like a spa treatment. I didn't want to think about how terrible I must look. We could still see Grayson and Tyler but they had grown smaller. They were climbing the embankment and walking around in the space where my Granddad's deck should have been. Then they started climbing up the hill toward where Tyler's house should be. There wasn't even a road there anymore.

Something was so wrong. I felt myself shiver and started to tell Abbey that I was just cold so she wouldn't worry, but realized that she was sound asleep. I tried to squelch the feeling of panic that had me in its grip. For the next thirty minutes I sat very still and watched as Grayson and Tyler walked the rim of hill; finally coming back down, crisscrossing the field to the extreme right, and then to the left as they made their way back to us.

I held my finger to my lips as they approached so they wouldn't wake Abbey. Grayson shook his head to indicate their lack of progress. Tyler spoke quietly, and I could see the confusion on his face.

"There's no sign that a house ever existed over there. There's nothing. No debris. No plumbing or pipes sticking up. Nothing."

"Could you see anything from the top of the hill? Malvern in the distance?" It was the only thing I could think to ask.

Tyler shook his head. "Just more hills and fields like this."

"Are we dead?" To our surprise Abbey sat up, fully awake. I'm sure her question had already gone through all our minds, but it was shocking to hear it out loud.

"No, of course not, Sparkle Butt." Tyler reached down and ruffled her hair. "Look, Danni is still bleeding. Dead people don't bleed." He turned to me. "I'd better take another look at that." He squatted and tightened his t-shirt tourniquet. I shivered again.

"So what do we do next?" I tried to think of what Dad might do in a situation like this, but drew a blank.

"Well, I'm hungry." Abbey slid off the rock and looked around. "Where's my backpack?" She asked Grayson.

"Sorry, Abbey. I left it back at the swimming hole. Be right back." He disappeared down the trail and the three of us waited in silence. There didn't seem to be anything to say.

Grayson reappeared in a few minutes with the pink backpack. "It's pretty wet." He shook it off and handed it to Abbey. To our surprise, she unzipped it to reveal that it was stuffed full of granola bars, peanut butter crackers, and fruit roll-ups. I remembered what Myra had said about them not having regular meals. This must be how they ate most of the time.

Grayson squatted next to her as she rifled through her stash of goodies. His brow had that deep worried look again.

"Were you running away, Abbey?"

"No." She shook her head innocently.

"Then why do you have all this stuff in your backpack?"

"Pax said we were going on an adventure and I needed to bring snacks."

Grayson looked at Tyler and then at me. Whatever was happening seemed to have something to do with Abbey's imaginary friend. Grayson took a deep breath.

"What else did Pax say, Abbey? Did he tell you where we were going? What kind of adventure?"

"No," Abbey shook her head. "Here's one for you and one for you and one for you." She doled out the granola bars with great efficiency and then opened one for herself.

"Thanks, Abbey." Tyler went ahead and opened his and took a bite.

"Thank you." I said even though I couldn't even think of eating anything. I slipped it into the pocket of my hoodie which was quickly becoming too hot. I took it off and tied it around my waist, trying not to be self-conscious about being in my pajamas.

"You should probably eat something." Grayson had noticed that I didn't open mine.

I nodded. "I will in a minute."

Thankfully, Abbey interrupted.

"I'm thirsty!" She said with her mouth full of crunchy stuff. She definitely needed something to drink.

"Well, I just might be able to help with that, Sparkle Butt," Tyler said quickly. "Hang on." He disappeared down the trail, but was back in just a minute carrying some of the empty plastic bottles that had been discarded in the gully.

"There used to be a spring right up here somewhere." Tyler headed down the tree line, and we all followed. I tried not to put too much weight on my wounded leg. It was really stinging.

"A little creek used to feed the swimming hole. It dried up when the development went in, but we may still be able to find a trickle. Here. I think this is it." He pushed aside some brush at the edge of trees and crawled underneath.

"Careful." Tyler called back. "There's some briars there."

The tangled vines had created an archway. Once we slipped underneath, it opened up into the forest again, and sure enough, there was a small stream of water gurgling out of the ground. Tyler rinsed off a bottle, filled it with water and gave it to Abbey first and then we passed it around. It was delightfully fresh and clean tasting. We all had seconds.

Abbey tugged at my hoodie like she wanted to tell me something.

"What sweetie?" She tugged again and I leaned over to hear her.

"I have to go." She whispered, but I knew the guys heard her, too. Tyler was trying not to laugh.

"Oh. Well okay. Here." I took her hand. "Um, guys, we are going to take a little walk."

"Let's go this way." Abbey pulled me across the little stream and on into the woods.

"Don't go too far." Grayson called after us.

"We won't." Abbey replied before I had the chance. I was a little concerned because she had broken free and was running ahead.

"Abbey wait."

"Here. See. This is good." She had found a nice little clump of brush that offered plenty of coverage although Grayson and Tyler were already well out of sight. I felt around in my hoodie pocket and found some tissues for us. I had put them there days ago before I left Los Angeles.

Los Angeles, I thought. It seemed so far away.

What is happening? This had to be some kind of dream but it seemed so real. I stood up and looked around. The forest was serene. The trees were huge and old and welcoming, and the air smelled of old pine needles and rich dirt. Birds were chirping overhead, and dappled sunlight danced around me as the branches swayed in the slight breeze. Even after all we'd been through, our surroundings felt almost magical. I walked a little further into the woods.

"Wait, Danni! I'm not finished." Abbey said anxiously.

"It's okay, sweetie. I'm just looking around. Take your time. I'm right here."

"Okay."

A few steps further and the forest seemed to change. I couldn't quite make out what the difference was, but the trees seemed to shift. I was sure it was an optical illusion, but the trees looked like they were planted in a row.

"Hey! Abbey, Danielle, where are you?" Grayson's voice was nearby and he sounded worried. In my mind's eye, I could imagine his handsome face with the furrowed brow. Abbey emerged from the bushes still struggling with her pants.

"We're over here!" She called back to her brother.

"I thought I told you not to go too far."

"A girl needs her privacy!" She yelled back. I had to laugh. One minute Abbey was all little girl and then she would say something that sounded like she was at least thirty years old.

"Hey guys. Look at this." I wanted them to see the trees. "It's odd." I walked a little further and stopped in amazement. The trees were definitely in a row – two rows, in fact.

There was a road in the forest! It was just a dirt road covered with a lot of leaves, but it was too wide and straight to be an accidental trail; not to mention the trees appeared to have been planted to line the sides so that their branches created an arch over the center. It was definitely that way on purpose. The strangest part was that the road seemed to start right where I was standing. Abbey came running up beside me and she stopped too.

"Grayson! Look what Danielle found!" Grayson and Tyler emerged from the trees not far from us. I could see the look of disbelief on both their faces as they got closer.

"What is going on?" Tyler's whispered question was genuine and wasn't meant for anyone in particular.

"This hasn't been here?" I asked in surprise. I was sure that he and Terry had probably ventured into the woods on occasion.

Tyler shook his head. "No. Until a couple of years ago, my family came camping here every year. I would have seen it. This…this is new."

Only it wasn't new. The road looked very, very old. It would have taken years, decades even, for the trees to have grown this way. We stood there quietly for a moment, letting the magnitude of the mystery sink in.

"Well, I'm just glad there aren't any yellow bricks anywhere." Tyler's voice sounded so serious that it took me a minute to catch on. Grayson got it first, and he actually laughed. His smile lit up his whole face. It was like the sun coming out after a particularly gloomy storm; all the worry and weariness and shadows just disappeared. It only lasted a moment, but it was worth seeing.

"What's so funny?" Abbey leaned her head sideways to look up at her brother.

"Oh, we're just being silly," Grayson patted her on the head.

"So what do we do now?" Tyler was staring intently down the road. It went straight into the heart of the forest. "It's usually best to stay put so that a search party can find you, but…" his voice trailed off.

"But we seem to be the only ones here…wherever *here* is." Grayson finished the sentence.

"So… who's up for a walk?" Tyler almost sounded like he was joking, but both he and Grayson were looking at me to see if I was onboard.

I was surprised at how rational I felt under the circumstances.

"We should fill up the rest of those soda bottles with water." I glanced up through the canopy of leaves at the sun, which had begun its morning march across the sky. "It's probably going to be a hot day."

CHAPTER 6

I insisted on wearing the backpack because I knew that Abbey would get tired soon and need to be carried, and I was right. We had only been walking for half an hour before she started needing "horsey" rides. And now, two hours later, she had finally fallen asleep on Grayson's shoulder.

It seemed like a good time to mention something I had noticed.

"Guys, can you tell which direction we are headed?"

"Same as the sun." Tyler answered. "We're heading west."

"That's what I thought. It doesn't seem like there have been any curves or forks, right?"

"No, it's been pretty much a straight line since we started." I could hear the curiosity in his voice. I glanced at Abbey to make sure she was still asleep.

"In that case, I think the road is disappearing." I tried not to let my voice waver. I had noticed that the trees behind us seemed to be changing every time we stopped to let Abbey rest, so I had started paying close attention to our direction. If we were curving at all that would explain it, but we seemed to be walking in a straight line. The road behind us was simply vanishing – becoming forest again.

Both Grayson and Tyler turned back to look.

"So it seems." Tyler's tone was almost matter-of-fact. There wasn't much else to say. In our own way, we had all accepted that we were not in charge of what was happening anymore. Tyler was staring at me with a concerned look on his face.

"Why don't we take a break?"

I felt a big bead of sweat run down my face. A break did sound good. My leg had gone from painful stinging to all out throbbing about thirty minutes ago.

"Here." I untied the hoodie from around my waist and laid it on the ground so that Grayson could put Abbey on it. It felt good to unload the backpack for a minute, too. Even the warm water we passed around tasted great. I noticed Grayson was staring at me now.

"Did you ever eat anything?" He asked.

I nodded, but it was a lie. I felt too queasy to eat, but I would never let them know. The last thing that I wanted to be was the fragile girl that had to be taken care of. I could tell he didn't believe me.

"Let me take a look at your leg again." Tyler said as he knelt down beside me and loosened the bandage.

"Mmm," he tightened it again. "You are probably going to need antibiotics."

There was no point in saying anything. We all knew that the chances of that happening were probably nonexistent.

"Pax says we should be there soon." Abbey startled us all as she sat up and stretched. "Can I have a roll-up, Danni? I want strawberry, please." I looked at Grayson and he nodded.

"Sure." I found one and handed it to her. "So, has Pax told you where we are going yet?"

Abbey shook her head and popped the whole rollup into her mouth, but she made an earnest effort to answer.

"No, but he said we should hurry now."

Even though I felt terribly overheated, a cold shiver ran through my body. There was an ominous overtone to the message. I could see that Grayson and Tyler were taking her seriously, too. Whatever was happening, Abbey's imaginary friend seemed to be a huge part of it.

"Well, then," Tyler was trying to sound nonchalant. "We'd better get a move on, don't you think?" He helped me up but refused to let me take the backpack. I didn't put up a fight. After Abbey had some water, we headed out.

We had walked for about twenty minutes or so without saying much when Grayson spoke up. "Is it me or does it seem to be getting lighter? I think the trees are thinning out." He was right. His artist's eyes had noticed the subtle change in light.

"Maybe we'll be out of the woods soon." I tried to make it sound positive, but I felt true fear at the thought of what might lie beyond the safety of the trees' shelter. The forest seemed to surround us with a gentle, protective kind of magic. It was almost as if it were its own person – a fairy godmother protecting us, first from the horrible storm, then giving us water, and now protecting us from the hot sun. It felt safe here.

I shook my head to clear my thoughts. Enchanted forests are for children's books, I reminded myself as I watched Abbey skip along happily in front of us. I tried to stay focused, but I felt like part of me was drifting away. I stumbled and Grayson reached out to steady me.

"You okay? We can rest again if you need to." There was genuine concern in his voice which embarrassed me. I was determined not to seem helpless. "No, no. I'm fine. Thanks."

A few minutes later, Abbey squealed with delight and started to run on ahead.

"Abbey! Stop!" Grayson demanded in a tone so stern it brought her to a standstill.

"But look!!!" She pointed, frozen in her tracks but still wiggling with excitement. Not far ahead of us, the woods abruptly stopped and the road continued out into an open field. We were about to walk right out of the forest. Grayson caught up with Abbey and picked her up.

"We have to be careful," he said gently, "We don't know what's out there. You stay with me. Okay?"

"Okay." Abbey put her arms tightly around her brother's neck. That worried little frown had settled on her forehead again. Grayson looked at me and then at Tyler. A bead of sweat rolled down my back as another slid down the side of my face. If I had felt better, I would have been mortified at how awful I must look. I could feel my hair sticking to my neck like a wet mat. My leg had gone from throbbing to all out burning, but I couldn't let that slow us down. We needed answers. We had to keep going.

"Let's do this." I heard myself say as I mustered all my strength and stepped out on my bad leg. I nearly vomited at the pain. I was glad to take the lead so that Tyler and Grayson couldn't see my face as I tried not to cry.

It was only a short walk to the edge of the woods, and when we got there, no one said a word for several minutes. Even Abbey was silent. The view was unbelievable. The trees had given way to rolling hills, with carefully laid out fields that were divided by hedges and rows of small trees. Several beautiful swans bobbed gracefully on a series of nearby ponds that shimmered in the sunlight. But it was what lay beyond the fields and ponds that had stunned us into silence.

The road wound in and out of sight as it dipped and curved up to a hill in the distance – and perched on top of that hill was a massive castle, complete with towers and turrets and battlements. I've seen castles in movies and history books and story books, but never one quite as majestic as this.

Abbey finally drew in a sharp breath and had the courage to ask, "Is it real?"

"I don't know," Grayson answered truthfully.

"It looks real." She countered.

"It does." Grayson nodded.

"Can we go see?" She was almost whispering.

Grayson glanced over at me and Tyler. "I think we have to."

I nodded and felt the landscape waver with the movement, making me want to throw up again. Grayson looked from me to Tyler with unspoken alarm. I vaguely understood that the look was because of me but I was finding it harder and harder to concentrate.

I think I have a fever.

I wasn't exactly sure if I said that out loud or if I just thought it. My pajamas were sticking to me like they had just come out of a washing machine, making me miserable.

"Maybe we should hang out here and rest until the sun moves on over. It's still a long walk, and we are almost out of water." Tyler said kindly.

"I don't think we have to worry about that." Grayson's voice was flat. He had been staring at the castle and I followed his line of sight. Even though it was still a long way off, the movement at the front of the castle was unmistakable. There were at least a dozen horses and riders leaving the castle gate at full gallop – and they were heading down the hillside toward us.

I turned my head gingerly to look back at the forest and felt the world spin around me as I did. I wasn't surprised to see that the trees had already moved again, completely disguising the road we had just been on. The guys saw me looking and glanced back, too. Our eyes met. There was no place for us to go. The road from the castle led right to where we were standing and stopped. There was no doubt that the riders were coming for us. I saw Grayson tighten his grip on Abbey.

It's okay. The enchanted forest has brought us here.

I must have actually vocalized this last thought because all three of them were looking at me strangely. There was no time to try and explain my feverish ramblings. The horses and riders had disappeared briefly behind a hill, but now they reemerged and were much closer. The massive horses were glorious at full gallop – taller than any horses I had ever seen – and the riders were majestic too. The rider in front was dressed in a tunic and vest with dark britches and boots. A cape attached at his neck had caught the wind and it sailed along behind him, revealing that his enormous shoulders were covered in metal armor. He looked almost mythological with long brownish-blonde hair and braids woven in on either side.

The other riders were dressed in a similar fashion – all slightly different, but equally stunning. All I could think about was how hot they must be. But then again, they looked like they lived at a gym so they were probably used to sweating a lot. Some of the riders were dark-skinned and several were women. The women were as jaw-droppingly beautiful as the men were handsome. One woman had long red hair that radiated in the bright sun, another was blonde and pale. None of the riders were wearing helmets, so maybe this was some kind of welcoming committee. At least I hoped so.

There was nothing to do but stand there and wait for them to arrive, which they did in a matter of minutes. Before the lead horse had even stopped, the rider in front threw his leg over and dismounted in a slide that deposited him right in front of me. He immediately dropped to one knee and lowered his head as all the other riders stopped behind him, forming two rows with their horses.

Oh my goodness, this man is gorgeous. What is he doing? Get up! I wish Kim were here, she would swoon. He's definitely her type! I truly hoped that I had not said that out loud. I glanced at Grayson, Tyler, and Abbey and was relieved to see that they were focused only on the entourage in front of us.

In a movement that made us all jump, the man and all the riders suddenly pounded their chest with their right arm in a type of salute. It was done in perfect unison and made quite a thud.

The man lifted his head and looked at me with exquisite blue eyes.

"Your Royal Highness, I am Arthmael, Defender of Geilgess. Permit us to escort you and your companions to the castle."

"Told you." I heard Abbey say in a sing-song-I-knew-it-all-along voice.

I almost laughed and probably would have except that I was having difficulty getting a good breath. This had to be some kind of prank – some elaborate ruse. There had to be a camera somewhere. I was from LA after all – entertainment capital of the world. But as I looked around all I could see were the serious, expectant faces of the riders and this handsome man kneeling before me. I realized that everyone was staring at me – waiting for me to say something. But what?

I tried to take a breath and then I felt it happen. It was shocking and frightening at first – the realization that I was about to pass out. It all seemed to happen in slow motion. I could see Tyler reaching to try and help me, but I was already falling forward. I was vaguely aware that the man who called himself the Defender of Geilgess was going to catch me, then darkness crept into my vision from all sides like a thick black ooze and filled in everything until even the bright castle on the hill was blotted out.

CHAPTER 7

I'm not quite certain of the order of events after that. When I opened my eyes again, I was aware of being held by Arthmael and we were on horseback at full gallop toward the castle. My eyes were sticky with sweat. I struggled to look backward to see if Grayson and Tyler and Abbey were okay but I did not have the strength to lift my head.

The handsome warrior with the chiseled face glanced down at me.

"Stay with me, Princess." His voice was tinged with concern.

Something is terribly wrong with me, I thought. *I can see it in his face.*

And then the strangest thing happened. As we galloped by the ponds, the swans all took flight. Even in my feverish state, it was quite an amazing sight. I guess I had never thought of swans being able to fly because they are such large birds. They surrounded us like an escort on either side.

I must have slipped into unconsciousness again because I was suddenly aware of being jostled and handed down to someone. I was no longer able to open my eyes, but I heard strange voices and broken bits of words as I faded in and out of reality. Someone was talking about "poison," another about "intention." It made no sense. Then abruptly my mouth was forced open and a horrible tasting liquid was poured in. I sputtered and tried to reject it, but I was going to have to swallow it or choke. The minute it went down my throat, it was like a brain freeze all over my body – icy cold pain spread to every pore. And then there was sweet nothingness.

I was happy to be back on the steps of the long lost house looking at the sea of little blue flowers in front of me. I sat down on the top step and let my legs dangle. The stone was warm – just right to sit on. I gazed at the flowers and wondered about the people who had lived here before the fire. What had they been like? By the looks of the columns on either side, it must have been a large and elegant home.

Had the fire destroyed all their dreams?

I was aware that the boy had joined me on the steps. It wasn't even necessary to look at him.

"Did you know them?" I asked, already knowing the answer.

"Yes."

"Did they survive?"

"Yes," he hesitated, "although maybe not all in the way you mean."

I was going to ask him to explain, but my attention was drawn to a large group of white butterflies that descended onto the blue flowers all at once. It was a beautiful event. There must have been thousands of them, creating a kaleidoscope of white and blue movement as they flitted from flower to flower. One of the larger ones fluttered my way and I extended my hand. To my surprise it landed on my finger and for a second or two I got to admire the intricate patterns of its gossamer wings.

"How does a caterpillar turn into something so wonderful?" I spoke my thought out loud.

"It must want to fly so much that it is willing to change," the boy replied.

It took me a minute or two to get my bearings when I opened my eyes again. I was lying down, that much I knew, but I didn't immediately understand where I was. I was looking up at a lovely weaving of green and gold leaves that alarmed me at first because it encompassed my entire view. And then I realized that it was the underside of a canopy bed. Everything that had happened came rushing back to me. I sat straight up with a start only to discover that I had been relieved of my muddy pajamas and was now wearing a thin strapless slip of a gown. I reached instinctively to my neck. The key was still there. I sighed with relief. Without Macaroni, it was the last thing I owned from my dad.

It was only then that I started to take in my surroundings. I was on a large velvet-covered bed situated along the wall of a room that was possibly the most ornate, luxurious, overwhelmingly beautiful place I had ever been. The entire downstairs of my granddad's house could have fit into it nicely.

On the wall directly across from me was an immense tapestry depicting swans floating on a lake. A lovely, graceful swan wearing a crown of gemstones was featured as the central figure. The pastoral theme continued all down the walls with painted murals that were inset between rich, ornate, wooden columns. I leaned out over the edge of the bed so that I could see better, and realized the columns were actually designed to look like the trunks of trees whose limbs reached high into air and became the beams that supported the vaulted ceiling. The ceiling was painted like a delicate blue sky with pink-tinged clouds. Even the soothing green velvet of my bed covers and the flowers woven into the canopy and draping were meant to give the impression of a forest refuge.

"Wow." I sounded lame, but I had to say something out loud. The room was just too magnificent not to acknowledge so I said it again with whispered awe. "Wow."

"There you are, Princess." The voice made me jump. It belonged to a tall dark-haired woman who had just entered from a small door at the far end of the room. She was a mature lady wearing a black floor length dress that resembled a uniform. Her hair was braided and tucked under a white cap. She quickly laid down the armload of clothes she was carrying and curtsied before she approached me. Even from across the room, I noted that her face seemed kind.

"You gave us quite a scare, Your Highness." She had an accent – but I wasn't sure if it was British or Irish – or maybe Scottish. It was something recognizable at least.

"How do you feel?" There was genuine concern on her face.

I had a thousand questions rush into my mind all at once.

"Where am I?" I blurted out, realizing it was probably rude not to answer her question, but I had more pressing things on my mind.

She just smiled kindly and answered in an expectant and dignified way. "You are at Castle Geilgess, Your Highness."

I remembered the man on the horse saying he was the Defender of Geilgess. So I must actually be inside the castle now.

"Where is Castle Geilgess exactly? I'm sorry, I'm not familiar with it."

"Castle Geilgess? It is the Castle of the Bright Swan." She said that as though I should know what it meant.

"I mean, where is it located?"

She smiled again kindly, choosing her words carefully. "That is difficult to say, Your Highness. The

Regent should be here by nightfall. It would be best if we let the Regent explain."

"The Regent?"

She nodded and her voice was almost reverent. "Yes. The Regent will be able to answer all your questions." I could tell by the way she lowered her eyes that I wasn't going to get much more of an explanation than that. So I changed the subject.

"How long have I been asleep?"

"Oh, only a few hours. You needed the rest. You've had quite an arduous journey."

"Where are my friends?" I asked anxiously and she seemed to brighten at this question.

"They are just down the hallway." She motioned to an ornate wooden door tucked away between two of the columns. "They'll be delighted to hear that you are awake. I was just taking them some garments so they can freshen up for supper. I don't think the little one is going to last much longer without a bite of something. I gave her some porridge earlier, but that one has an appetite!" She gave a little laugh.

I found myself smiling back at her, thinking of Abbey and her backpack of snacks. I wanted to hop off the bed and run to the door to see her, but thought better of it since all I had to wear was a slip. I really wanted to see Grayson and Tyler too.

"Do you know where my clothes are?" I asked hopefully.

The woman smiled again knowingly. Her expression seemed as if she was reading my thoughts.

"They are being washed now, Princess. I'm afraid the water was necessary to cool your body down quickly."

It came back to me then. After the terrible liquid had been poured down my throat, I had been submerged in ice cold water several times. That would explain where all the mud and sweat went.

"I'll be right back to help you get dressed, Your Highness." She curtsied again and started to walk away, but I stopped her. It was time to address the obvious.

"Excuse me."

She turned to look at me expectantly.

"Yes, Your Highness?"

"I'm sorry. What is your name?" She seemed genuinely surprised and maybe a little pleased and embarrassed that I had asked.

"I am Winnow, my Princess."

It was definitely time to put all this Princess confusion to rest.

"That's just the thing, Winnow. I'm not a princess. My name is Danielle Taylor and I'm from Los An...,"I stopped, realizing I wasn't really from California anymore. "I mean, I've been staying with my granddad in Georgia – and I really need to get back there. We all do. I'm sorry, but there's been some sort of mistake."

Winnow smiled warmly and brightly. "No mistake, Your Highness." She was choosing her words very carefully again. "Where you are now, is not where you were. And here, in this place, a Princess is not born, she is chosen."

I had no idea what she was talking about but her words sent shivers up my spine. Was she saying that I had been chosen to be the Princess of Geilgess or something? It was a ridiculous notion – but looking at her face, I could see that there was no hint of deception in this nice woman.

I shook my head and started to protest, but she interrupted. "The Regent will explain everything, Your Highness. But if ever there was any question, the Arrow of Intent confirmed that you are, indeed, our Princess."

"Arrow of Intent?" I was becoming more confused by the minute.

"The dart that struck your leg. The poison is deadly if it's not treated right away. Only the true Princess of Geilgess could have survived as you did. You are meant to be here." She curtsied again with a look that indicated that she had said too much. She quickly moved to pick up the mound of clothes and scurried out of the room before I could even think of anything else to say.

Memories of the tornado, the sharp pain in my leg, Tyler pulling out the piece of stick and binding my wound, and the painful walk through the forest swirled through my mind. So it wasn't an infection at all. Someone had tried to kill me! I had to let that sink in for a moment.

I pushed back the slip to look at my leg and, to my amazement, it was almost completely healed – only a tiny red area remained where the stick – the dart – had gone in. How was that even possible?

The events of the day seemed like they had happened weeks, even months ago, and yet it was all just this morning. Three days ago, I was celebrating getting my braces off and having my first kiss, and now that seemed like a lifetime ago, too. So much had happened and none of it made sense.

Time flows differently here.

Even though the room was a comfortable temperature, I felt my body start to shake. I slid off the bed and hurried toward the big wooden door. I needed to find Grayson, and Tyler, and Abbey right now to make sure they were really okay.

I nearly tripped over the slip, which was longer than I thought. At that exact moment, some late-day sunlight suddenly came spilling into the room through windows that were high up on the wall. Everything around me had suddenly turned golden. The room positively glowed with beauty. It was like being in a serene cathedral. This really was a chamber fit for a princess. I couldn't explain it – but as I stood there, bathed in its beautiful light, I felt like I belonged.

Which, of course, was crazy. I needed to snap out of it. Fortunately, Winnow returned in a bustle and guided me to one of the tapestried chairs near an ornate dressing table.

"Here, let's take care of the hair first." She quickly detangled my hair which was still slightly damp and started weaving a ribbon through it. My back was to the mirror, but I was very curious and kept trying to see what she was doing with no luck. In a moment, she stepped back to admire her handiwork, smiled, and nodded.

"And now for the dress." To my surprise, she opened a panel on the wall nearby which turned out to be a closet with only one dress inside and it was exquisite. It was a ball gown in the palest shade of blue or green – or maybe it was silver – I couldn't tell. Kim would have given it some fancy name like "breath of the ocean in moonlight." It definitely had a magical iridescence.

I had to step into it so that Winnow could lace the bodice up from behind. It fit perfectly and snugly to the waist and then cascaded to the floor in a graceful swirl of light, flowing material. A lot of material. I could feel a crinoline underneath giving the skirt its poof. As Winnow fluffed out the bottom, I realized that it was much longer in the back.

Oh my goodness, I'm wearing a dress with a train! Kim would be going crazy right now!

Winnow stepped back and clasped her hands in approval.

"I knew that was the perfect choice for you." She finally allowed me to turn and look at myself and my mouth literally dropped open in surprise. There was a princess staring back at me from the mirror! Winnow had somehow managed to weave a ribbon of jewels around my head that gave the illusion of a crown without actually being one. It shimmered and sparkled with even the tiniest movement. Cinderella herself would have been envious of the dress. It was so beautiful. I truly looked like I belonged in a fairytale.

Winnow had gone back to the hidden closet for a pair of soft ballet slippers. She helped me manage the layers of skirt to get them on."One more thing." Winnow reached into the dressing table drawer and pulled out a long, wide, golden sash which she wrapped around my waist like a belt and looped in the front. Then she opened another drawer and brought out a golden brooch that looked quite ancient and attached it to the sash where it was wrapped. On its front was the figure of the crowned swan, obviously the symbol for the castle. This latest touch didn't go with the dress at all, but it suddenly gave the princess ensemble a much more regal appearance. It was the seal of this kingdom, of that I was sure. Looking in the mirror, the only reminder that I was Danni Taylor from Malvern, Georgia was the key around my neck.

I didn't know what to say as I stared at her finished work, so, of course, I said something stupid.

"Winnow, it's...it's beautiful. Do people really dress like this here just to go to dinner?"

Winnow smiled in her kindly way and said, "You'll be meeting with the Regent later, so it is best to dress for that occasion." She didn't give me time to respond. "Now, with your permission, Your Highness, I will check on the meal and return shortly to escort you to the Great Hall. Your friends are just through there." She motioned to the door. "They will be most happy to see you." And with that, she curtsied and hurried out of the room in the opposite direction, which seemed to be her way of doing things.

I swallowed hard. In this larger than life dress – maybe even because of it -- I felt very alone. All I wanted to do was run down the hallway to find Grayson, and Tyler, and Abbey, but something about the dress kept me from doing that. Instead, I carefully made my way toward the door. Kim had designed some costumes last year for our school play and she had said that the characters didn't really come to life until the actors put on their costumes. I could believe that. There was something about this ethereal dress with its train floating gracefully along the floor behind me that made me believe that some part of this strange adventure might really be true. In this universe – wherever it was –maybe I could be a princess.

The door opened into a small corridor that was just as lavish as the room. Columns on either side gave way to exquisitely painted beams that arched to form the ceiling. Stained glass windows on the right diffused the sunlight. I passed two closed doors on the left, and then I heard voices from the open archway ahead. The laughter was unmistakably Abbey's. I couldn't help but smile.

As I neared the opening, I saw that it was the entrance to a large sitting room. Murals lined the walls above a grouping of lavishly tapestried chairs and sofas. Abbey was in an alcove that contained a dollhouse castle. She was prancing a little wooden pony across the bridge over a make-believe moat – obviously to rescue the princess doll hanging out of the tower window. She had been given a perfect pink dress with roses at the waist, and her hair, like mine, sparkled with jeweled ribbons. She was definitely in her element, just chatting away to herself and her doll friends.

I looked around and saw Grayson and he took my breath away. He was standing near the wall admiring one of the paintings. He was studying it so intently that he didn't hear me enter. I was glad because it gave me a minute to compose myself so that I wouldn't drool or something equally embarrassing…he looked that good.

He had been dressed for the occasion as well. He was wearing black britches and boots, topped by a richly embroidered black belted tunic with capped sleeves. His undershirt, with its billowy sleeves, was black, too. With his long dark hair, he could not have looked more noble and at home in these surroundings.

"Danni!" Abbey's squeal of delight startled us both. She had discovered me standing there in the archway and came running. I bent to give her a hug and as I glanced at Grayson, I saw that he was looking at me the way I had just been looking at him. I felt color rising to my cheeks.

Abbey stepped back and looked up at me with teary eyes. "We thought you were going to die."

"I know. I hear I was pretty sick. I'm sorry you were so worried."

She smiled again and did a complete twirl in her pink princess dress.

"Do you like it?"

"I love it!"

"Me too! And look!" She went running to the castle dollhouse. "My very own castle!" Within seconds her attention had turned back to playing rescue-the-princess with her new toys. I glanced at Grayson, who was still looking at me in that way. I suddenly felt extremely shy.

"I'm glad you are okay." I was relieved that he spoke first. "How do you feel?"

I guess "you look nice" or "pretty dress" or something like that would have been too much to hope for from him.

"I'm okay, thanks. I'm sorry I scared everyone." I suddenly realized that I had not seen Tyler yet. "Where's Tyler? Is he okay?"

"Yeah, he's still changing."

"Did I miss anything? Do you know where we are?"

Grayson shook his head. "All I've heard is that we are in Geilgess and that someone is coming who can answer our questions."

I nodded. "Same here."

"Have you seen this?" He motioned to the far end of the sitting room where large velvet drapes had been pulled back to reveal a balcony with a thick marble railing.

"No." I could smell a wonderfully intoxicating scent on the breeze that floated in as I walked toward it, but when I stepped out onto the actual balcony, I had another one of those jaw-dropping moments. We had to be several stories up because the view was spectacular. The sun was poised to set and a large lake in the distance reflected the pinks and purples of the clouds, giving everything around us a charmed glow. A range of mountains provided a splendid backdrop for it all. On this side of the lake was a meadow covered in white flowers, which must have been responsible for the soft-as-petals fragrance that floated our way.

"It's beautiful." I murmured.

"It is." Grayson said softly. He was standing right beside me and part of me hoped that he was looking at me when he said it. Everything seemed so perfect – and strangely enough, perfectly normal. As if we had stood on the balcony before. Suddenly so easy and comfortable together. I took a deep breath and soaked it all in.

This is what happily ever after feels like!

The thought tickled my brain with delight and then embarrassed me. I quickly stepped forward to look over the balcony and was stunned to see how high up we really were. We had to be on the backside of the castle. A long, long way down, I could see the rock cliffs that the castle was built on and two massive culverts that funneled a river underneath the structure and then routed it down the hillside and on toward the lake.

"How did we get up here?" I stepped back.

"Well, you were carried. The rest of us took the stairs." It sounded like he was teasing, but I had to look at his face to be sure. He flashed that amazing smile that made me feel weak at the knees. I smiled back, then looked away quickly for fear that he would see how vulnerable I was to his charm.

"My apologies, but I've never been poisoned before."

"Poisoned?" His voice was genuinely shocked. I looked back up at him and saw that his whole expression had changed. A heavy scowl materialized on his forehead.

"I...I thought you knew."

He shook his head.

"Knew what?" It was Tyler emerging out into the last daylight on the balcony. He, too, had donned the obligatory castle garb and he wore it well. His outfit was similar to Grayson's, but done in browns and greens. He looked more like a hunter than a prince, but he was quite dashing in his own way. He let out a whistle when he saw me.

"Well, look at you, Princess! Sparkle Butt wasn't kidding!" I was glad it was getting dark. Hopefully my glowing red face wouldn't be too noticeable.

"You clean up pretty well yourself." I smiled.

"Oh, this old thing? It's just something I threw on." Tyler didn't miss a beat.

We all laughed at that.

"Tyler!" Abbey came running out and grabbed his hand. "Finally. Can we go eat now? Pleeeeease?"

As if on cue, Winnow entered from the far side of the room and with a quick bow called to us.

"If it please Your Highness, supper is served."

Abbey clapped her hands happily and ran to join Winnow. We followed. I was still getting used to the train and all the material around my feet. I hoped I wouldn't fall flat on my face in front of everyone.

Entering the hallway outside the sitting room was like walking into another world. It was so huge that twenty people could easily have walked abreast. It was done entirely in two tones – white and gold. The floor was white marble with golden inlays. Each side of the hall was lined with golden columns that were designed to look like vines that linked to each other to create a series of archways, and then climbed up several stories, crisscrossing and linking overhead to form a graceful golden latticework across the ceiling.

The hallway was lit by numerous ornate chandeliers, but it was what was happening on each side as we walked along that was completely magical. Forest scenes had been sculpted in white and gold relief, then inset underneath the side arches so that they were visible mostly in silhouette. As we moved, the sculptures seemed to come alive and move, too. A deer raised its head to look at us. A bird flitted from tree to tree. A squirrel hopped along the ground with a nut in its paws, a breeze stirred the leaves. It was an utterly enchanting play of light and form.

Abbey reached up and took my hand.

"The forest." She whispered in awe.

I nodded and squeezed her hand, glancing over at Grayson. He was completely intrigued by the art and animation that surrounded us. I could tell that Tyler was a little wary of it all. I was too, but it was hard not to be drawn into its beautiful spell.

Winnow stopped at the end of the hallway and I realized that this corridor gave way on the right to a massive curved staircase that led down to a huge dining hall. From the landing, we could see the whole room. The dining table ran down the center and could easily have seated fifty people in its elegant velvet chairs. Food had already been placed at one end of the table – overflowing bowls of fruit, breads, butter, cheeses, nuts, and pastries that all looked sumptuous in the dancing candlelight. Before Grayson could stop her, Abbey bounded down the stairs. I was pretty hungry myself and might have done the same thing if it hadn't been for the dress. I was grateful when Tyler offered me his arm. I was so glad that I didn't trip on the way down.

I had to sit carefully and with the straightest posture ever because of the tight corseting of my dress. No wonder royal people always looked so aristocratic in pictures -- they didn't have a choice. I sat next to Abbey – who had to perch on her knees to be able to reach the table; Grayson and Tyler sat opposite us.

It was another amazing room with tapestries that ran down the walls on both sides, depicting one long scene of the forest in misty twilight. Beautiful orbs of gold had been woven into the fabric in a line, giving the appearance of a procession of people moving through the trees with lanterns. I felt that if I looked long enough, I would be able to make out one of their faces. It was a wonderful abstract illusion. Grayson, the artist, couldn't stop looking around. He was like a kid in a candy store.

Winnow stood near the table until we were all seated and then she curtsied and said, "I will go make ready for the Regent now," and she was out of the door before we could even say thank you.

"Is it just me, or does it strike anyone else odd that in a place this size, there only seems to be one person working?" Tyler had a point.

"Well, there were the Defenders." I replied. Even though I had been sick, I couldn't forget the beautiful people on horseback who came to rescue us.

"True." Tyler conceded.

"Maybe we just caught them in the off season." I couldn't tell if Grayson was joking or serious. An awkward silence descended upon us as we all looked at each other. Everything seemed different, softer and surreal in the misty glow of the candles. Were we dreaming? What was happening to us? It was Abbey who brought us back to the present. She folded her hands and said a little prayer.

"Thank you for the food God, and for keeping us safe, and for new friends. Amen."

"Well said, Sparkle Butt." Tyler reached for a piece of bread and the spell seemed to be broken. For the next thirty minutes or so everything seemed almost normal. If you took away the clothes and the castle, we were just four kids having a fun meal together. Abbey entertained us with a very dramatic re-creation of my fainting spell complete with eyes rolling back in her head and her tongue hanging out. She had us all laughing until it hurt. As I looked around I realized that the three of them had probably had many meals together like this and that I was just filling in for Terry, the lost sister and girlfriend, but it still felt good to be a part of their little group. A couple of times I even caught Grayson looking directly at me as if he were studying me. I looked away quickly, hoping my embarrassment didn't show.

Suddenly Abbey let out a shriek that took us all by surprise. We were on our feet in seconds. I tried to grab her as she slid out of her chair and made a dash toward the far end of the table. We all saw him at the same time. A young man had stepped forward from the shadows. He was tall and pale with an interesting, angular face and the lightest crystal blue eyes I had ever seen. Abbey stopped just a few feet from him and did a curtsy. He in turn took a deep bow. It seemed like a routine they had done many times.

Abbey turned to us excitedly. "I told you he was real." I knew immediately that he was her imaginary friend. The one who walked with her in her dreams. I knew also that he was the boy in my dreams, too. As I approached him he bowed again.

"Your Royal Highness." He murmured as our eyes met.

"Beauty for ashes." I responded. His words had stuck in my head.

He smiled and bowed his head again. "You remember."

"Yes." I smiled.

"I am honored."

"You know him?" Grayson sounded incredulous.

I nodded. "From a dream."

"This is Pax." Abbey took his hand and beamed happily because we could now see the friend she had been talking about so much. "This is my brother Grayson and my friend Tyler."

"It is an honor to make your acquaintance." Pax bowed again. I could tell it made Tyler and Grayson a little uncomfortable because Pax appeared to be our age.

"So you've been visiting them in their dreams?" Tyler's voice was full of caution.

"I am a Dreamwalker." He replied gently. "Well, an apprentice." He added quickly.

"Well, Pax, we would really appreciate it if you'd answer a few questions for us." Tyler started to go on, but Pax interrupted.

"Forgive me, but I am here to escort you to the Regent, who will be able to answer all your questions much better than I could ever hope to."

I had a sudden queasy feeling in the pit of my stomach. We were really going to meet this Regent person and find out what was going on. Part of me wanted to know and part of me was terrified.

Winnow's voice at my elbow made me jump.

"Your Highness, I was wondering if perhaps Lady Abigail might like to join me. We've put together a puppet show just for her." I didn't have to look at Grayson to know that he was scowling. Abbey clapped her hands in delight. I wanted to ask who "we" was referring to, but Winnow didn't give me a chance. It was as if she read our minds.

"Our very existence here is to protect and serve the court. I can assure you that no harm will come to her." It was an odd statement, but I had no doubt that Winnow was telling the truth.

"Please, Grayson?" Abbey pleaded.

I could see that he believed Winnow, too. His face softened and he nodded. It was obvious that the meeting we were about to have was not suitable for a child. I felt that gnawing anxiety in the pit of my stomach again.

"A puppet show! Yay!" Abbey grabbed Winnow's hand and after a quick curtsy from Winnow, they headed for the staircase with Abbey practically dancing with excitement.

"I'll see you in a little while." Grayson called after her, his voice tinged with worry.

"Okay," Abbey called back, but they were already to the top of the stairs and out of sight. Grayson let out a slow measured breath. The four of us were left staring at each other awkwardly.

"If you'll follow me." Pax turned and headed to the other side of the dining hall. There was a small door in the far corner of the great hall that opened up into another long corridor. This hallway had none of the magical elements we'd previously encountered. It was ornate, but in a very serious way. Marble statues of Defenders -- like the ones who met us at the edge of the forest -- lined the walls at intervals. Each one had a drawn sword pointed upward, creating a walkway of salutes to whomever might be passing through.

Pax stopped halfway down the corridor and indicated that we had reached our destination. It was an odd room that required us to duck our heads and step down to enter. None of the lavishness of the castle was presented here. It was a room made entirely of smooth old stones – the floor, the walls, and the arched ceiling– everything was made of stone. It was lit with torches positioned around the perimeter. In the center of the room there were five very large high backed chairs arranged in a circle facing each other. The chairs were made entirely of stone as well. Something about this place made me think of King Arthur's round table – only minus the table. Without a doubt this room was ancient. I got the sense that the castle might even have been built around it.

Wars have been planned here.

The thought gave me a cold chill. I turned back to ask Pax about its history, but once again found myself speechless as I watched him assist a stunning woman who was stepping down into the room to join us. Her hair was long and silver white, but she was not old. Her face seemed to shimmer, making it almost impossible to tell her age; she actually appeared to be glowing from within. She was dressed in a floor length white gown covered by a glorious cloak the color of the blue flowers in my dream. Every inch of the cloak was embroidered with a symbol or swirl of stars. She wore a full crown that glittered with large stones that matched the robe.

"May I present Her Imperial Majesty, Queen Avazdenia; Princess Regent of Geilgess."

Pax bowed low as she passed him, and to my complete surprise, I responded with a curtsy. I wasn't even sure why I did it, but this woman was magnificent and she was an Imperial-something after all; it just seemed appropriate. I felt a little stupid and I wasn't sure if I did it right, but I noticed that Grayson and Tyler both bowed stiffly, too. She smiled and tilted her head forward in a slight acknowledgement as she approached. To my surprise, she reached for my hand. Her fingers felt cool and warm at the same time.

"Let us be seated," she said as she led me to one of the chairs. "We have much to discuss, yes?" We waited until she was seated to lower ourselves onto the cold stone chairs. She was every inch as regal as her name implied with her royal robe tumbling to the floor around her. I turned again to look for Pax, but he had disappeared. I wondered if someone else would join us to sit in the fifth chair.

She tilted her head to look at me closely. I noticed her eyes were vibrant green and as she studied me, she blinked very slowly and visibly. She was like us – but not. Her gaze was intense and probing.

"At long last the Princess of Geilgess has been chosen. Welcome child." Perhaps it was my fancy dress or simply my weariness from the day's adventures, but I suddenly felt bold.

"Forgive me, Your Majesty, but my name is Danielle Taylor. Everyone here keeps calling me the Princess, but there has been some mistake. I...we are from Malvern, Georgia in the United States...on Earth," I fumbled, "And we need to go home." I immediately wished that I had kept my mouth shut.

The Queen seemed to completely ignore my statement. She looked at Grayson and Tyler with that same penetrating stare, then back to me. Her face had lost its smile and when she spoke it was with great seriousness. Her voice seemed to reverberate off the walls of the stone room.

"I understand that the events of the day must have been disquieting, and I will do my best to answer all your questions; however, you must understand that heaven and earth has been moved, quite literally, to bring you here. I cannot even begin to explain the honor that has been bestowed upon you. It is, of course, your right to refuse the title and be returned to your former existence without fulfilling your destiny here, nevertheless, I find it difficult to believe one chosen for this office would do so."

I felt my cheeks burn partly from the reprimand and partly from anger. How dare she scold me when I didn't even know what was going on! I glanced at Grayson and Tyler for help but they both had strange expressions on their faces – as if they knew more about what was happening than I did.

I was already sitting perfectly straight because of the dress, but I raised my chin as I met her gaze.

"Then perhaps, Ma'am, you would be so kind as to tell me where 'here' is. I would also like to understand how we got 'here,'" and who, exactly, chose me to be the Princess. I would also like to know who tried to kill me."

Tyler physically jerked at my last sentence, and then I remembered he had not heard about the poisoned dart yet. He looked at Grayson, who was scowling and leaning to one side of his chair, not looking at either of us.

Ironically, the queen seemed very pleased with my reply. "Spoken like a Princess," she said with a smile. "As you have already perceived, the Kingdom of Geilgess exists in a different dimension than the one that you are familiar with."

"So it is real," I breathed the words out, not realizing that I had been holding my breath.

"Quite real. Had the poison from the dart succeeded in its mission...," she paused.

"I would be dead."

The Queen did not reply, instead she addressed my second question.

"As to how you got here, you arrived by means of a – convergence – yes, I believe that is the most appropriate word...the linking of great forces to create a pathway between worlds."

"The tornado?" Tyler had finally decided to join the conversation.

"Yes." The Queen nodded.

"My grandfather..." I choked up before I could say more.

"...Is safe and sound as are all your families. The convergence was designed for the four of you and the four of you only."

"So you're saying that Pax lured Abbey into the field, away from our houses, knowing we would follow." Grayson finally spoke up in an angry measured voice.

"Pax *is* a Dreamwalker." She stated the obvious as if that would somehow make things better.

"Who?" I felt my voice quiver. "Who has the power to do this – to create a convergence? To bring us here without our consent?"

The Queen tilted her head and blinked a slow blink as her crystalline green eyes narrowed on me in a very cat-like manner.

"Why you of course." She said quietly. "All of you played a part." She swept her hand to include Tyler, Grayson, and Abbey upstairs. "Together you created the catalyst for the convergence, but only a true princess," she paused and looked directly at me, "could have unlocked the pathway between our worlds."

Even though I was sitting on hard stone, it felt like the seat was falling away from underneath me. The whole room seemed to shift and spin. She was saying that I brought us here – that I had somehow orchestrated this journey. My brain scrambled for a defense.

"What makes you think that it's me?"

"Because, my dear, this is Geilgess. The Castle of the Bright Swan. Other kingdoms are ruled by princes, yes, but Geilgess has always and will always be ruled by a princess. It is the structure of things."

"Who makes these choices?" I asked the Queen bluntly. She raised one of her silver eyebrows as if she didn't understand my question, but I knew she did, so I pressed.

"You say that in this…realm… a princess is chosen for the crown, not born to it. By whose authority? Who decides who gets to be a princess or prince and who doesn't?" It seemed like a logical and fair question.

The Queen met my eyes with a steady gaze.

"Alas, that I cannot answer. Those choices are made by powers far greater than all of us. It is only up to us to decide whether or not to believe and accept the challenge and responsibility given to us."

I felt my face go red with anger. She was talking in riddles like a politician.

"The last Princess of Geilgess. Where is she?" I struggled to steady my voice. "What happened to her?"

To my surprise the Queen looked at Grayson. I followed her gaze and felt another wave of vertigo overtake me as his eyes met mine. They glittered darkly in the torchlight, and his face suddenly seemed cold and impenetrable yet electrifying like the first day I saw him. Sitting there in the high backed stone chair, he looked every bit as royal as the Queen. The only thing missing was a crown on his head and a robe over his shoulder, and the balance of power in the room could easily be shifted. As I looked at him, I realized that I didn't really know him at all.

There was something they weren't telling me. I looked at Tyler for help, but he avoided looking at me and stared at his hands. Total silence descended on the room as they seemed to wait for me to process the answer to my own question. When I did, I felt like I would throw up all over the ancient stone floor.

"The girl in the painting." I whispered. I was surprised that my voice even came out at all.

Tyler finally helped me out. "Grayson's dad saw you on the security camera." I felt my face burn at having been caught sneaking into the garage. So his dad had been home after all.

"I just wanted to see Grayson's work." I stammered to the Queen in my defense. "My granddad said he was really good. But that still doesn't explain what we are doing here."

"Her name," the Queen's voice took on an almost reverent tone, "is Kyna." As the Queen spoke all the torches in the room dimmed simultaneously and then flickered back to life. "She was the Princess of Geilgess for two years. She was about your age when she was chosen."

"What happened to her?" I was afraid to ask, but I knew that I had to. I could feel the Queen's eyes dissecting my every move so I tried to look as composed as possible, but I was shaking and I knew the Queen had to see it.

"She was given the Queenship of Ferrinwold. Her work as the Princess of Geilgess was so extraordinary that she was selected to receive the Burdens of Queenhood when she turned seventeen. A responsibility which she loyally accepted. Only…"The Queen stopped talking and for a moment a strange look came over her face, but then she continued. "Kyna was abducted on the way to her coronation. By whom, we do not know. Until now…perhaps." Her voice had a lingering question mark tucked inside.

She looked again at Grayson. He met her eyes without so much as a flinch. I had a hundred questions racing through my mind, but I was grateful when Tyler interjected his own question.

"Abducted by whom? There aren't any people here."

The Queen seemed a little annoyed, but she condescended to answer. "Most of the citizens of Geilgess live on the far side of the lake. It is a small kingdom, that is true – positioned for a transition such as yours. The castle will remain unoccupied until it is claimed." She looked directly at me as she said the last sentence, and then she continued.

"No one from Geilgess would have done such a thing; however, Ferrinwold is a larger, prosperous kingdom on the far side of the Realm, and there are those who would lay claim to its riches. Just like the countries in your world, our kingdoms are sometimes beset by strife and war. There were many in Ferrinwold who did not want Kyna's influence – her goodness and good judgment – in their midst, and we believe they may have had substantial help from another empire not of this realm. You see," the Queen leaned forward to emphasize her words, "the battle of good and evil is not confined to your Earth."

I still had no idea what role we were supposed to be playing in all of this. To my surprise, Grayson reached into the pocket of his tunic and pulled out a small square notebook. Our eyes met as he leaned forward to hand it to the Queen. There seemed to be a hint of an apology in his expression.

The Queen accepted the notebook and carefully studied each page. I could see that it was a sketchbook with black and white drawings on each page. Toward the end of the book, the illustrations were splashed with colors here and there, but I could not make out what they represented. The Queen finally closed the book. Her face, which had glowed so beautifully throughout the meeting, took on a muted pallor.

"It is as we feared." She stated flatly and handed the book to me. My hands were visibly shaking as I reached for it. I could only assume that Tyler had already seen its contents. I seemed to be the only one in the dark.

The first few pages were unmistakably sketches of the forest road to Geilgess, then the castle and the swans. They were followed by drawings of the princess I now knew to be named Kyna. She appeared lovelier with each illustration. Grayson had captured the sheer beauty and nobility of the girl the Queen has described. Then abruptly the drawings took on a dark muddled appearance with a hideous winged creature that looked part dragon, part worm splashed across the page. On the last page, there was a preliminary sketch of the painting I had seen in Grayson's garage, of the princess chained to a wall.

My hands were shaking so badly that I lost my grip and the book fell with a clatter to the floor. Tyler quickly slid off his chair to retrieve it. I could see that he wasn't sure what to do with it, so he handed it back to the Queen. He didn't look at me and neither did Grayson -- which was probably a good thing. I wanted to cry but that seemed un-princess-like, so I pushed my feelings down until I could control my physical shaking and focus on the Queen.

"What does any of this have to do with me?" I asked, forcing my voice to be cool and contained.

"Kyna reached out across the universe and found someone who could hear her pleas for help." The Queen turned and handed the sketchbook back to Grayson. "Grayson, there is not a seer or holy man in the entire realm that has been able to accomplish what you have done. You have great powers that must be developed. Pax has traveled through oceans of dreams in the hopes of even a glimpse of something that would give us a clue to what happened to Kyna. When he finally saw her likeness in the little one's dreams, he knew that forces were at work to restore to us what was lost."

"So you can go get her now?" I was still trying to make sense of all of this. "You can tell where she is from Grayson's drawings?"

The Queen looked at me and blinked one of her slow blinks. Her face registered a mild surprise that I still didn't seem to understand what was going on. I didn't. She was going to have to spell it out for me.

"Thanks to Grayson's drawings, we do know now that she was taken from our realm. A convergence will be necessary to bring her home."

"That's great news!" For the first time since we entered the room I felt a glimmer of hope. "How many royals – princes and princesses and queens and kings are in this realm? If you combine forces you should be able to create a wormhole big enough for an army to go through and rescue her." I thought of gallant Arthmael and his band of Defenders. I had no doubt they would volunteer for the mission.

The Queen did not answer and another silence fell over the room. I looked at Tyler and Grayson and felt the blood drain from my face. I saw it in their expressions before the Queen finally responded.

"This challenge was given to you, Princess Danielle of Geilgess. Only you and the companions you brought with you can go forward to complete the mission. It is what you were chosen for."

I was numb with horror as I remembered the four of us huddled in the abandoned swimming hole while the tornado passed over us – sealing our passage and our shared destiny.

The Queen startled us by standing up suddenly. I managed to stand up although my legs felt like jelly. Grayson and Tyler stood up quickly, too.

"More than this, I cannot tell you." It was apparent that our audience with her was almost over. "The fate of Kyna, Queen-elect of Ferrinwold, is in your hands." The Queen turned to leave and surprised me by reaching out to touch the key on my necklace. She started to say something, but Grayson interrupted.

"What if we refuse?" I was surprised to hear him challenge the Queen. I thought this must have been what he wanted all along. The chance to rescue the beautiful maiden.

The Queen gave us one last sweeping glance.

"Then you can return to your home and Geilgess will soon only be a memory of a dream you once had." The Queen headed toward the door, where Pax had suddenly reappeared to assist her. He must have been standing outside the whole time. He bowed deeply and then extended an arm to help her step up. She stopped, but did not look back.

"And the Princesses of Geilgess will be no more."

Her words echoed off the stone walls with a terrible finality. Then she left and the room suddenly seemed empty and dark and small. Her incredible blue robe, which trailed for yards behind her, quietly slid out of view. Pax made a slight bow in our direction and followed her -- leaving us standing there staring first after her and then at each other.

I felt so stupid. For some reason I thought I knew Grayson and Tyler – that I had connected with them and they had accepted me. This was all my fault for trusting them so easily – for wanting to belong. The tears that I had submerged were coming dangerously close to the surface. Grayson noticed and took a step toward me. He had a tortured look on his face but I didn't care. I stepped away quickly.

"Danielle, I know what you are thinking, but you must believe that I didn't know any of this was going to happen." Grayson faltered for a second and then went on. "I kept getting these strong images in my mind and I started sketching them. That's all, but the more I did, the stronger they became."

"It's true, Danni," Tyler came to his friend's defense. "He's been drawing the same things over and over for months. After the tornado – when the houses disappeared – we – we suspected that they were somehow linked, but we couldn't be sure and how crazy would that have sounded if we tried to explain it?"

I didn't even make the effort to formulate a response. The reality of everything that had happened was weighing me down like an anchor. I was finding it hard to breathe. I realized I didn't even know who had tried to kill me. I needed to get out of that room. Somehow I managed to move. I maneuvered my skirts and train and used the doorway arch to pull myself up into the corridor.

"Danni!" I wasn't sure if it was Tyler or Grayson that called after me and I didn't care. I was running back down the Hall of Defenders. I found the small door that opened up into the dining hall. It was dimly lit now and no longer felt warm and inviting. The huge tapestries along the wall seemed dark and frightening. I felt like the faceless people carrying the golden orbs that were so carefully woven into the fabric had all stopped just to stare at me. What a worthless choice for a princess, they must be thinking.

I could feel my beautiful dress floating along behind me as I ran across the marble floor. I grabbed the front of my skirt as I reached the stairway and managed to scramble up the steps without incident. I hurried down the fabulous white and gold corridor without even looking at the enchanted forest animations. I just wanted to find the doorway to the princess chambers...and do what, I asked myself? Hide? I didn't know. I just wanted to feel safe.

The door to my room was unmistakable – marked with a swan carving that matched the brooch Winnow had attached to my sash. I pushed it open and felt relief to be back in the sitting area. The velvet curtains were still pulled back and I could see a full moon glistening in the night sky. I tiptoed out onto the balcony and was once again gripped by the beauty of this little kingdom. Below me, fireflies were floating gracefully above the fields and the bright moonlight doubled its glow by rippling across the lake. That lovely fragrance that I had smelled earlier still sweetened the air, and in the distance I could see the lights from the village that the Queen had mentioned. There really were people who lived here. People who needed a princess. A brave and noble princess like Kyna – not someone like me.

I turned back into the room and headed down the hallway. I assumed Grayson and Tyler would be returning shortly and I didn't want to see them right now. One of the doors down the corridor was open and I was relieved to see Abbey sleeping soundly in a trundle bed – worn out from all the excitement of the day no doubt. Winnow was sitting in a chair nearby – performing the role of the dutiful babysitter now. She had fallen asleep, too, with her head nodding forward, emitting a slight snore with each breath.

I tiptoed past Tyler's room and slipped back into the princess chambers only to experience another breathtaking moment that lifted me out of my misery for a few seconds. I had no idea how it had been accomplished, but the firefly motif had been brought indoors and the walls of the room were aglow with tiny flickering lights that resembled the fields outside. I glanced up at the vaulted ceiling and it, too, was awash with twinkling lights that were designed to look like stars in the night sky. It was absolutely magical.

I made it halfway to the dressing table before hot scalding tears forced their way out. I sat down on the cool floor with my princess dress poofed out around me and sobbed. The impossible events of the last two days swirled through my head. I just wanted to go home. I wanted to be in my own bed in Los Angeles talking to Kim until midnight about clothes and kissing Jack Corbin. As much as I loved Granddad and Myra, I wanted to get as far away from Malvern, Georgia and Grayson and Tyler as I possibly could. Abbey was sweet, but I could never be the big sister she lost, and I wanted all these queasy happily-ever-after feelings about Grayson to go away because he had turned out to be just a good-looking jerk after all. Tyler was nice, but he was still in love with a dead girl. There was no place for me in their world.

And I certainly didn't belong in Geilgess…this beautiful, magical, fairytale realm. I still couldn't even be sure if it was real or not – but I remembered the feeling of the poison racing through my body and it was hard to invent another explanation. It seemed very real. And if Geilgess was real, it desperately needed a heroine. I couldn't even begin to fathom how to be that person. No, I didn't belong here. I wanted to go home.

I wiped my face and made my way to the dressing table. I was relieved to see that my pajamas and hoodie had been returned and were carefully folded in the chair. My shoes were on the floor, too, all nice and clean. At the same time, their presence felt almost like a question mark, as if I was being asked to choose which world I wanted to be a part of.

I carefully took off the brooch and sash and returned them to their drawers, and after a few minutes of fiddling with the ties at the back of the dress, I was able to wriggle out of it. I couldn't figure out how to open the wall closet panel so I carefully laid the dress over the chair and pulled on my comfy pajamas. I put on the hoodie too, even though it was a warm night. Maybe I would start to feel like myself again once I was safely back in my own clothes.

All I felt was tired. The stress of the day enveloped me like a heavy coat and I was glad to go curl up on the green velvet bed, but the minute I closed my eyes my mind immediately went to Kyna. The thought of her chained to the wall in that horrible place made me sick. This had been her bed – her kingdom for two years. Where was she from? How did she get here? What had she done to distinguish herself enough to be chosen to be a queen? Were we really her only hope of rescue? I couldn't turn the questions off – I had far too many to even think of sleep.

None of it made any sense, of course, but Queen Avazdenia had made it clear that it was my responsibility to find the answers. Surely they didn't expect me to arrive in this world fully prepared to launch a rescue in a foreign land. Maybe this was some kind of Princess boot camp…a training exercise. I deliberated that notion for a moment before discarding it. There were too many factors that would make it impractical, the least of which involved Abbey, Grayson, and Tyler.

I wondered if Grayson and Tyler were back in their rooms now, and if their minds were buzzing with questions like mine. I wanted to believe that Grayson had been in the dark about what was going on but it didn't excuse the fact that he and Tyler had not included me in their speculations even after our whole world disappeared. I wondered what was happening now in Malvern. Was Granddad worried or did he even know that I was gone? Time and space definitely felt different here.

The questions continued to spin around in my brain until I was too exhausted to consider them any longer. I could finally feel the land of dreams sucking me in. I wondered if Pax would be there. If he was, I had a few things to discuss with him.

CHAPTER 8

I don't think I slept very long. When I awoke, the room was awash with moonlight that had found its way in through the high windows. The chamber was even more enchanting in this silvery glow. I sat up in amazement as I looked at the tapestry that, by day, had depicted a crowned swan floating on a lake. Now, in the moonlight, it revealed two figures standing at the far side of the lake in silhouette, a young couple facing each other, holding hands and poised for a fairytale kiss.

That could have been me and Grayson.

I pushed the thought from my mind and slid out of bed. There was no time for romantic notions now. That could be any couple, anywhere. It was just an illusion after all.

The castle was completely still. I padded over to the dressing table where my beautiful princess dress sparkled like treasure in the moonlight. I caught sight of myself in the mirror and realized I still had the jeweled ribbon in my hair. It, too, shimmered in the half light. I carefully unwound it and laid it with the dress. I would not be needing it where I was going. Not that I knew exactly where that was.

I pushed the skirting aside and picked up my sneakers, but decided not to put them on just yet. I didn't want them squeaking on the marble floors. I was surprised at how calm I felt...I think I had already made the decision before I fell asleep, but now there was no doubt in my mind that there was only one course of action for me.

Somewhere there was a girl – a girl not much older than me -- chained to a wall imprisoned by hideous and evil creatures. I had a choice to do something about it or not. And even though the Queen had said that if I chose to do nothing and return home, I would forget about all of this, I knew that on some level what happened here would remain with me forever. I couldn't even explain to myself why I felt that way, but my gut was telling me that the choices I made now were somehow determining my destiny.

My dad had continually risked his life for people he never knew, and ultimately, he had died because of it. He was far braver than I could ever be. I did at least have a girl's face and her story –some of it anyway -- and the knowledge that my actions might prevent a great evil from gaining power over a serene and peaceful place. Even here in this mystical dimension the battle between good and evil raged on, and someone, somewhere thought I could make a difference.

I had been chosen. I had to try.

I opened the door and tiptoed down the hall. I didn't want to wake Tyler or Grayson or Abbey. Whatever role they had played in this – it was not their fight. Tyler's door was slightly ajar and I could see that he had flopped sideways across his bed and was fast asleep on his stomach.

Grayson's door was open, too. He had fallen asleep in a sitting position on the bed, his tall, lean frame barely fitting onto the small mattress, which was probably meant for a lady-in-waiting. Abbey was still asleep in the trundle looking like a little angel without those big pink glasses covering her face.

There was no way that I could ask any of them to do this with me. Grayson and Tyler needed to protect Abbey and get her back home. Unseen forces had brought us together, but the Queen had made it plain that I was the one with the responsibility for rescuing Kyna and restoring order to the Realm. I forced my legs to move. If I stood there looking at Grayson for much longer, I would lose my resolve to go.

The sitting room was very dark. The drapes had been pulled to close off the balcony and only one small sconce lit the room. I carefully opened the door and hurried down the Hall of Enchantment. That was the name I had given the magical animated forest corridor outside my chambers, although in the dimmed lighting most of the carved animals appeared to be still and sleeping. I did notice an owl's head turn and follow my movements. I would love to meet the artist who designed this place.

I stopped at the top of the stairway above the dining hall and sat down to put on my sneakers. My plan – if you could call it that – was to find Arthmael and get some sort of weapon. I was guessing that the Defender's quarters were somewhere on a lower level of the castle. I just had to figure out how to get there. I was hoping the hall with all the statues of Defenders might offer some clues.

I hurried down the stairs and across the vast dining room which was downright spooky in the semi-darkness. I groped around and found the little door in the corner which gave entrance to the large passageway we had used earlier for our meeting with the Queen. I was thankful that it was still well lit by the torches spaced between the saluting statues. I was drawn to each beautiful and noble face as I passed. This hall was an obvious tribute to all the warriors who had died to protect the kingdom, and the lights were never dimmed.

I kept looking for the door to the room where we had met with the Queen but couldn't find it. I was sure I was in the right place, but the door had simply vanished. Castle Geilgess was full of secrets. There was nothing to do but keep going. It was a long hallway, but my hunch paid off. It ended in another downward flight of stairs, this one much smaller and winding. I took a deep breath. There was no turning back now. I was descending into the belly of Castle Geilgess.

The stairwell reminded me of a lighthouse that I had once visited with my dad, only this time I couldn't see the bottom so I had no idea how far I had to go. Around and around I went, thankful for the little brackets of torchlight that appeared just when it seemed that I was moving into complete darkness. I was about to give up on reaching the bottom when I abruptly found myself on a platform face to face with an ancient-looking door.

There was a large metal crossbar holding whatever was on the other side at bay. It took all my strength to lift it from the latch and I had to jump out of its way as it swung downward with a loud clatter. So much for stealth mode. I pulled hard on the handle and the door finally lurched open with a screeching wail as though it had not been unbolted in many years.

I made just enough room to slip out and found myself in a large stone courtyard. The full moon overhead was like a brilliant light bulb bathing all the stones in a silvery glow. I turned to look back at the castle and was astounded at its enormity from this level. I had to step back and crane my neck to see the top. I had descended to this level from one of the highest turret towers.

"Wow." I decided that I definitely needed a better vocabulary, but for now "wow" seemed to be working. I took a few more steps backward and said it again before I could stop myself. I was like a tiny speck compared to the immensity of the castle walls.

"It's pretty amazing, isn't it?"

I let out a little scream before I realized that the voice belonged to Pax. He had been standing in the shadows by the tower, but now walked toward me looking a whole lot like a ghost in this weird lighting.

"I'm sorry, Your Royal Highness," he said gently and bowed deeply. "I startled you."

"No," I was going to try and save face but thought better of it. "Well, yeah, a little. What are you doing here?"

Pax was standing very near to me now and I could see that his translucent eyes were actually glowing. He was in his element. He belonged to the world of the night and shadows and dreams. He smiled and I realized that he was actually very handsome in his own way. There was a charisma about him that seemed to beckon me to move closer. I wanted to step away but could not.

"You asked me to come." It took me a few minutes to stop gazing into his eyes and realize what he was saying.

"Oh." I finally came back to reality and put two and two together. I had managed to fall asleep for a few minutes back in my room. I must have asked for his help in a dream – but for what I wasn't sure. "Sorry, I don't remember."

"It's this way." He turned and headed across the courtyard. I had to walk quickly to keep up with his brisk stride. I could hear horses snorting somewhere nearby so the stables must be close.

"Is it weird for you?" The question came out of my mouth before I could stop it.

"Your Highness?" He stopped so quickly that I almost tripped over him.

"Could you maybe just call me Danni? I mean, you have been inside my head already. All this formality seems unnecessary, don't you think?"

Pax laughed and turned to look at me and I almost screamed again. His eyes had become even more radiant with hypnotic light. He almost looked like a different person. He turned away quickly and continued to walk, only slower.

"If that is what you wish…Danni."

"Thanks. I just meant…it has to be strange being in other people's dreams." Open mouth, insert foot, but I forged ahead. "Dreams are weird enough if they are your own. I can't imagine having to move in and out of other people's dream states." He stopped again and looked down at me in a way that made me both fearful and fascinated. His eyes blazed with cool crystalline fire.

"It is…amazing." He said finally after searching for the right word. "And it is terrifying. And sometimes…it is beautiful." His answer and the way he was looking at me gave me goose bumps.

"Over here." He continued across the courtyard toward a low stone structure. All I could do was follow. He ducked underneath a darkened archway. I couldn't see and bumped into him as he unlatched a hidden door and shoved it open.

I had absolutely no appropriate expression for the sight that met my eyes, so I remained silent. This had to be the armory. It was dimly lit, but Pax grabbed one of the torches near the entrance and walked around lighting other torches until the huge room was completely illuminated. It reminded of the room where we met with the Queen – ancient stone arches and floors. The walls were lined with all manner of weapons and armor – strange looking metal masks with empty eyes, breastplates, and metal boots and gloves were all on display and ready to wear.

The room had a strange smell that was unfamiliar to me. I felt frozen in place at the threshold, as if actually stepping into the room would seal my fate. I had no idea what I was doing or how to do it. My brain was screaming at me to run away as fast as I could. Pax must have sensed my desperation because he was suddenly by my side, eyes flashing bright silver.

"Pax," my voice trembled and I clutched at his arm for support. "I don't know about any of this stuff. I don't think I can do this."

"You," he said leaning close, "are Princess Danielle, Chosen One of Geilgess. That makes you Archpraelia of the Defenders."

"Archpraelia?" I stammered. I had never heard that word before.

"Princess Warrior."

"What?" My head was spinning. What was he saying?

"The fact that you are here is in and of itself a miracle, Danni. Don't you see that? Can't you feel it?"

I couldn't answer. I didn't know how. Just a few days ago I was worrying about what to wear on the first day of school. None of this made sense.

Pax pulled his arm away and stepped back.

"Only you can decide what you will believe in." He said quietly, and before I could stop him, he was gone, leaving me there in the doorway to choose.

I must have stood there a long time before finally stepping into the room. Everything that Pax had said was still rattling around in my brain. I was trying hard not to be terrified of the stands of armor and their helmets with the empty eyes. I made myself focus on the wall with swords. There were so many. How would I ever know which one to choose?

And then I saw it. It was smaller than the rest and shaped almost exactly like a grown-up version of the little dagger that I had used when Dad and I played pirates. It had been placed high up on the wall and even on tiptoe I wasn't able to reach it.

"Here, let me help."

I gasped. It was Tyler. He had to stretch, but he reached over me and managed to grab the sword. The minute he placed it in my hands I knew it was the right choice.

"Tyler, what are you doing here?"

"Well, you didn't think I was going to let you have all the fun, did you?" He was trying to be flippant but didn't quite pull it off. He turned and started looking through the armament on the opposite wall and pulled down an archer's bow and quiver of arrows.

"Do you know how to use those?" I asked, surprised.

"Junior State Champion three years in a row." He winked at me as he slung the pouch over his shoulder and secured it. He was still wearing his castle garb and he looked right at home with the arrows on his back and a bow in hand. I looked down at my pajama shorts and bare legs in dismay. As if he were reading my mind, Pax came striding back into the room with some clothes in one hand and boots in another. He handed them to me.

"They belonged to one of the stable boys, but they should fit," he said apologetically. I took my hoodie off, hung it on the wall, and pulled on the scratchy britches and shirt over my pajamas. After everything that had happened, there didn't seem to be any point in trying to be modest. At least the boots were worn and comfortable, and they might offer a little protection. Tyler helped me secure the belt for the dagger around my waist and I practiced sliding it in and out.

"Do you know how to use that?" It was his turn to ask me.

"My dad taught me a few things, I guess." I didn't mention that it had been seven years ago while we were playing pirates in the backyard.

"He taught her well. Everything he did was to prepare her for this moment." Pax had been standing quietly watching us. I swung around to face him.

"You knew my father?" I was breathless. Had he visited my dad in his dreams?

Pax's eyes had almost returned to normal, but they took on a somber glow as he replied. "He was a great and noble man." He shut his mouth tightly and I could tell by his expression that it was pointless to ask him for anything more. He followed some Dreamwalker code of honor.

"There's some smaller armor if you want to try it," he quickly changed the subject.

I shook my head. "This is a rescue mission, not a battle. We need to get in and out quickly and quietly."

"So what is the plan, Princess?" Tyler made an effort to smooth over the awkward silence. He tried to sound gung ho, but inside he must be dreading this as much as I was.

"Don't you start, too!" I attempted to sound annoyed, but I realized that I was quickly growing used to being called a princess. Perhaps it was because I was being asked to take the lead and make decisions. Those decisions had been easier when it was just me, but now there was Tyler to think about. His face had grown quite serious. I know mine had, too.

"I think...," I looked from Tyler to Pax for confirmation. "I think the road will lead us to where we are supposed to go – just like it did in the forest."

Tyler nodded in agreement, but Pax remained motionless and silent, making it plain that I was on my own now.

"So let's do this." Tyler held out his hand for a fist bump and I bumped him back. My legs felt wobbly as I headed for the door. Tyler and Pax followed. I ducked under the arch and back out into the courtyard and came to a stunned halt.

The whole area was filled with horses and riders. The Defenders were all there, dressed in full battle armor that gleamed fiercely in the moonlight. The men and women riders were indistinguishable now. Each one had on a helmet with a metal piece that ran down their nose to protect their face. I realized that the design was another tribute to the swan. Like everything else at Geilgess, even the armor was a form of art.

It was an awe-inspiring sight and I could feel my heart racing as I watched the horses stomp and pace. I turned to Pax, but as usual, he had vanished. Tyler and I were standing arm to arm. It was just the two of us now.

One of the Defenders came striding toward us. He removed his helmet and dropped to one knee. Even with his head lowered, I immediately recognized Arthmael – my hero from this morning.

"My Princess." Immediately all of the Defenders saluted with a strike to their chest. With their armor on, the sound was thunderous.

"Arthmael. I didn't get the chance to thank you for saving my life. Have you come to my rescue again?"

Arthmael stood up slowly. I had forgotten how larger than life he seemed.

"The Defenders will escort you to the boundaries of Geilgess, Your Highness. Beyond that we are not permitted to go. We will be waiting there for your return."

"Thank you." I said to all of them as well as Arthmael.

One of the Defenders on horseback leaned over and handed Arthmael the reins to his horse. He put on his helmet and mounted so swiftly that I was taken off guard when he reached down and scooped me up to sit in front of him. His massive arm circled my waist and pressed me tightly to his chest. Tyler quickly jumped on behind one of the other riders and just like that, we were galloping at full speed through the courtyard and across the bridge. The sound of the horse's hooves on the stones was deafening until we reached the soft dirt road.

It was a heady feeling. All my senses seemed incredibly heightened. I tried to take in everything. The smell of the horses mingling with the smell of flowers on the wind and the meadows around us outlined in silver by the light of the moon. I glanced back at the castle and noted that there were lights coming from some of the upper windows and I wondered if Grayson was awake yet. Had he even realized that we were gone?

I was right about the road knowing the way. It continually materialized in front of us and I realized that we were heading away from the castle in a different direction than we had arrived. Everything got darker as a cloud passed over the moon. Our horses slowed to a careful walk. The riders carrying torches moved forward to flank us and lead the way. I was just getting used to the rhythm of riding when one of the horses ahead of us suddenly reared up with a snort, and Arthmael's horse halted and jerked. Arthmael gripped me tightly as he reined in the stallion.

"The Midnight Forest," his voice was near my ear. His tone cause me to shiver.

Of course there would be a Midnight Forest.

The moon had reappeared and I could see the barren, twisted tree trunks that announced the woods just ahead of us. This was not a welcoming forest. A mist floating along the ground picked up the moonlight and gave the whole scene an eerie Halloween-ish glow.

I was holding onto Arthmael's arm tightly, but I already knew that this was as far as he and the

Defenders could go. The rider who was transporting Tyler sidled up beside us. It was too dark to make out Tyler's expression and I was glad because I knew my own face must be frozen with fear.

"I guess this is our stop." I tried to sound brave, but my voice cracked and trembled. Tyler had already slipped down and he helped me dismount. Arthmael followed and we watched as the entire guard backed up and moved into a defensive line behind us.

"Arthmael. Something tried to kill us…me…when we came through the convergence to get here. Do you know who it was?"

"A mercenary of the highest order," his voice was filled with disgust. "They are trained to sense the shift in energy as a convergence is created and they move quickly to carry out whatever task they have been hired to do."

"It is dangerous work," he added. "If they are pulled into the convergence, there's very little hope of survival. They prefer to skirt along the rim and see how much damage they can do from there."

"Sounds like a coward to me." Tyler's voice was guarded.

He's as scared as I am.

My mind was in high gear. That meant if we did succeed in rescuing Kyna, there was still the possibility that a mercenary "of the highest order" could be waiting to strike. I looked back at the line of Defenders. Behind them on a distant hill I could just make out the castle.

They were positioned with their shields up, ready to protect the kingdom against any intruder. I couldn't explain it, but I felt a sense of kinship toward them. I felt better knowing that if someone or something did try to come back with us, they were here to stop it.

I could sense that they were waiting for me to say something, but I was sure if I tried it would come out wrong.

What do you like to do?

Grayson's question from yesterday morning raced through my mind unexpectedly. I felt like I had lived many lifetimes since then. I surprised myself by turning back to the line of Defenders. A hush immediately fell over the field. I was literally quaking in my boots as I walked forward and looked at the small army in front of me. I couldn't see their faces, only their helmets shining in the moonlight. I refused to let my voice show fear.

"My father was a...a Defender in my...world." My voice was a little shaky but I felt a new strength as I thought about my dad. An approving murmur ran through the ranks. "He used to tell me that I had to strive to be special every day. I had forgotten what that meant until I came to Geilgess. Thank you." I couldn't think of anything else to say. There was another low rumble of voices as I turned back to face the forest.

"Princess Danielle!" The cheering that erupted behind me both startled me and filled me with courage. I turned to look back at them one last time.

"For Geilgess!" I raised my arm in a fist just like I had seen warriors do in the movies. The response was nothing short of thunderous. "For Geilgess!" they roared. I turned quickly back to Tyler. He immediately fell into stride beside me as we headed back to Arthmael at the front.

"Now that's what I call getting in touch with your inner princess," he teased. "I like it."

"Shut-up." I was a little embarrassed, but glad that I had done it.

"No, it's good…really."

One of the scouts approached us and offered us his torch, but Tyler quickly shook his head.

"No thanks, we've got it covered." He reached underneath his tunic and pulled out my flashlight. I had forgotten all about it.

"The flashlight! You still have it!"

"Yeah, I thought it might come in handy. It's a good one, too. The indicator says we've got about nine hours of battery life left."

I smiled, thinking of how Granddad had probably made sure it was fully charged and ready to go for me. I missed him terribly but I couldn't think about that now. "Let's hope we don't have to use it all." I said quietly.

A hush fell over the field again as we approached the place where the road had ended. Arthmael was waiting there, his face unreadable in the half-light.

"Your Highness." He bowed and to my surprise pulled his sword. At the same time everyone in the regiment did the same thing. All swords were drawn and raised just like the statues in the Hall of Defenders in the castle.

"We await your return, My Princess." He said boldly.

We all heard it then. The sound of the grass crinkling and moving as the road started to form again. And up ahead in the Midnight Forest, the tree limbs had started to move as they made way for us to enter.

This is really happening.

"I think that's our cue." I could hear the fear in Tyler's voice now.

I nodded. It was time to go.

CHAPTER 9

We discovered quickly that the flashlight wasn't really necessary. The bright moon overhead provided enough light for us to see through the ghostly mist that was hovering over the ground and parting perfectly to create a path for us. The barren trees on either side had formed a tunnel – their limbs twisted into grotesque shapes that glowed green with clumps of algae. At least I hoped it was algae. We had to be careful not to trip over the gnarled roots that jutted out into the trail.

Behind us we could hear tree limbs moving and we simultaneously turned to look back. The Defenders were already disappearing behind the tangled branches – the glow of their torches was our last connection to Geilgess, and to Grayson and Abbey. The sight brought to mind the tapestry in the great dining hall with its line of glowing orbs. Was this what it was depicting?

"We can still go back. There's still time to change your mind." Tyler said, his face distorted in this strange light, giving his features a craggy, sunken look. I was grateful that his voice at least sounded normal and kind.

I shook my head. I knew that I had to keep going. But he didn't. I tried to think of some way to let him off the hook. I swallowed hard.

"Tyler, I can't explain it, but I feel like this is something I have to do – but you don't have to come with me. The Regent-lady made it plain that I'm the one who is supposed to do this. We…this could be dangerous. We don't know what we are walking into."

"There's no way I'm letting you do this by yourself." Tyler turned back to the path and started walking. I was flooded with a sense of relief and moved quickly to join him.

"Thank you."

Tyler shrugged in an effort to make it seem like it was no big deal.

"It'll be an adventure we can tell our grandkids about." I wanted to hug him for trying to sound so nonchalant – like this was the most normal situation in the world. I wondered if he and Terry had ever talked about getting married and having children. Maybe they had even picked out names. Kim and I had spent many late nights discussing what our futures would be like right down to the kind of houses we wanted to live in and how many kids we would have.

We had been walking in silence for a few minutes – lost in thought about things that might never happen when the sound of the limbs thrashing brought us back to the present. We both turned and Tyler switched on the flashlight, but it was just the forest moving once more, determined to wipe away any traces of the path we had been on.

It was doing a good job. There were no more glowing orbs in the distance – just the moon, the trees, and us. We were deep in the woods now and the cool air was rich with the smell of ancient dirt and leaves. The unearthly mist that had been swirling around our feet had dissipated and the path ahead of us beckoned bright in the moonlight, flanked on either side by the Midnight Forest's misshapen sentries.

"Why do you think this is happening, Tyler?" My voice came out in a whisper for no reason. I couldn't quite make out his expression as he tilted his head to look at me, but I could see the moonlight reflected in his eyes.

"I don't know, Danni." He turned back to the path and I was struck by how handsome and strong he looked in profile. "I've been trying to figure it out and none of it adds up."

"I know," I said as we started walking again. "I keep thinking I'm going to wake up but then something else happens and it all seems so real. My head keeps telling me it's impossible but I don't have any other explanation."

"You know my mom works with your granddad over at Hadley Aerospace. She's a Quantum Physicist and she would say that the chances of this kind of thing happening are extremely high. She would say it is not only likely that it happens, but that it probably happens more often than anyone realizes."

"She works with Granddad? What does she do?"

"I've never really been able to figure it out. She has tried to explain it but then I ask too many questions and she says that it's classified and that if she tells me…"

"She'll have to kill you?"

Tyler laughed. "How did you know?"

"Granddad said the same thing to me yesterday – or was it the day before – I can't remember now." I felt a pang of homesickness for Granddad. "Time feels different here, doesn't it? It's like we've always been here."

"Yeah. It's strange. This is where my mom would start talking about something called the Planck Scale or Quantum Entanglement."

"She sounds really smart."

"Yeah. She is pretty amazing. I obviously took after my dad." He laughed, but I could hear a tinge of pain in his voice. He had lost Terry and now his dad had left. I decided to go ahead and say it.

"Granddad told me what happened. I'm sorry that…" I was in too deep to stop. "I'm sorry about your dad."

Tyler was quiet for a moment and then he let out a measured breath.

"Thanks. It's been tough – for Mom especially – but we'll get through it. Hey, I'm sorry about your dad, too. He's a legend in Malvern, you know. A real hero. He saved all those people."

It was my turn to swallow tears. I cleared my throat.

"Thanks. I miss him a lot." I reached up to touch the key on my necklace. "Maybe your mom is on to something. Sometimes I feel like he is so close – like if I go in the next room he'll be sitting there waiting for me. Do you ever feel that way about Terry?"

"No, but that's okay. It would hurt too much."

My heart cramped and I instinctively reached for his hand. He didn't pull it away and for a few minutes we walked hand-in-hand in comfortable silence.

He's definitely one of the good guys.

After all he had been through he was here in this mysterious, desolate forest trying to help me and keep me safe. I wanted to kiss him on the cheek, but instead I let go of his hand. We had reached an embankment and I scrambled up ahead of him.

"Whoa."

On the other side of the rise, the forest parted to reveal a large circular glade. Our path seemed to go straight into the center of the clearing and stop.

The moon suddenly slipped behind a cloud and I felt a drop of rain. We both looked up and saw dark clouds racing across the sky.

"The convergence?" I asked, trying to hide the fear I felt gripping my chest.

"I think this might be it."

We made our way down the other side of the embankment and out into the open. The wind had definitely picked up and lightning sliced the sky in the distance. A bolt of thunder followed. My impulse was to duck, but I knew that it was pointless. We were here, after all, to hitch a ride.

I had never felt as vulnerable as I did at that moment. Standing in the center of the field in the middle of the night at the path's end, waiting for this monster of a storm to overtake us, was almost unbearable. It took every ounce of courage I could muster to keep from running. I could tell that Tyler was terrified, too. He unexpectedly pulled me close and wrapped his arms around me tightly and put his head on top of mine. His toned muscles were like rock, and I could feel his heart pounding with adrenaline.

The lightning and thunder quickly surrounded us, and even though the wind and rain were slashing at my face, I forced myself to keep my eyes open and watch as a column of light descended and enveloped us. It finally became too bright and I gratefully buried my face in Tyler's chest, and that's when I felt the ground fall away. We were floating in a brilliant wind tunnel. Dad had taken me for indoor skydiving lessons when I was eight and this was the same sensation. I was grateful for Tyler's steel grip around my waist and I prayed that whatever was happening to us did not include a mercenary with poisoned darts.

And then it was over. More quickly than it had started, the light disappeared and we fell to the ground with a thud. The moon had disappeared altogether leaving an inky black sky behind. I could barely see the outline of Tyler's face.

"Are you okay?" Tyler was checking his quiver and bow and I was feeling for my dagger.

"I'm okay." I lied. I was wet and shivering and terrified. "You?"

"I'm good." He lied, too.

Thankfully a faint, colorless light was beginning to appear at the edge of the sky. I hoped that it signaled the arrival of morning and not something far worse.

As our eyes adjusted, we discovered that we were in a meadow of sorts. It was decidedly different terrain than the field we left. There were low-lying shrubs around but the tall grass and trees had completely disappeared. Even the Midnight Forest would have been a welcome sight right about now.

How will we get home?

I wasn't going to let myself think about that now or I would panic. I forced myself to focus on our situation. Maybe the light on the horizon was coming from a town.

A strange noise caused me to stop breathing for second so that I could hear more clearly. There it was again – a metallic banging sound in the distance. It was happening at precise intervals.

"Do you hear that?" I asked, but I could already see that Tyler heard it too.

"It's coming from beyond that hill," he nodded.

"Let's check it out."

Tyler nodded in agreement.

"Stay low. Let's try to make it to that big clump of bushes up there." Without even thinking about it I had given an order and Tyler gave me a thumbs up.

For the next half hour we moved in short little bursts across the field staying as low to the ground as possible and finding bushes, clumps of grass, or rock formations as stopping points. The strange clanging noise had stopped, but we still got down on our bellies and inched our way up the hill. I was so grateful for the clothes Pax had given me. They were scratchy but not nearly as scratchy as this rocky terrain would be on bare legs.

Tyler inched up to look over the crest of the hill first. He slid back down quickly.

"This is bad," he whispered.

"What?" I whispered back.

"I can't…you'll have to see for yourself."

I carefully inched up to look over the crest of the hill. It wasn't at all what I was expecting, although I couldn't really say what I thought I might see. In the distance, barren, rocky, mountains were jutting up against a lavender morning sky, and situated in the foreground was a small castle-like fortress of dark stone. Compared to Castle Geilgess it was a tiny structure, consisting of only four short turrets topped with embattlements that stood out in silhouette against the growing light. The towers were designed around a central recessed area – obviously to guard it. I could just barely make out a barred window in the middle section.

I shuddered. Kyna could be chained up in that room.

I slid back down and huddled next to Tyler. It was going to be light soon. We needed a plan.

Tyler surprised me. "Grayson drew that."

"The towers?" I stammered. "I didn't see them in the book."

Tyler shook his head. It was getting light enough for me to see his expressions now and the look on his face scared me more than anything we had already been through.

"Before the book," he continued shakily, "when he first started drawing this…" he hesitated, searching for the right word,"…this world. His studio was filled with sketches of this place. I thought it was for a graphic novel he was working on, but he threw most of them away. And then he started seeing Kyna in his dreams."

"Is he in love with her?" I was shocked by my own question. It had nothing to do with getting out of our situation alive, but it was a question that kept creeping into my mind.

"Kyna?" Tyler sounded as surprised by my question as I was. He shook his head. "I've known Grayson since third grade. He's never been one to talk about things. I don't know. All this started about the time that...about the time of the accident. I think at one point he thought he was losing his mind. I was worried about it, too. We all were. The guilt was just eating him alive."

"Guilt? I don't understand. Was he driving that day?"

"No, that's just it. He was supposed to be driving, but he bailed to stay home and draw. So he blames himself. He's sure that if he had been driving that day, Terry and his mom would still be alive."

"That's horrible."

"Yeah. That's when the really strange drawings started. Just not his style, you know? Before then, he was doing all these amazing superhero sketches – and they were really, really good. I mean *really* good. There were some publishers in New York that were interested in hiring him. And then, all of a sudden, he's drawing castles and dragons and beautiful princesses. It was a big departure – and he was obsessed – working on the illustrations all day and all night."

I could see how it must have seemed like Grayson was going over the edge, but I couldn't think about him now as much as I wanted to. I forced myself to think about our present situation.

"Is there anything that you can remember about the drawings that can help us now? Anything about the fortress?"

Tyler was silent and his silence said more than words ever could have.

I started to ask again when we heard the strange bonging noise resume, only this time it was louder and much closer. Tyler stiffened. I started to push myself up to take a peek when Tyler grabbed my arm.

"If this is what I think it is, it's bad."

"Bad?"

"If it's what Grayson drew, then it's real bad." His voice was like steel. Our eyes met and the warning in his expression was unmistakable. If he was right, whatever was about to happen was something terrible.

I nodded, trying to prepare myself as we both pushed ourselves up slightly to look over the top of the hill again. It was much lighter now. The bonging sound was coming from the top of one of the turret towers and I noticed movement at the base of the fortress near an opening on one side. Someone was coming out – or more accurately, it looked like someone was being shoved out. It was a man. He fell to his knees and rolled for a little bit. It looked as if his hands and feet were bound. He managed to pick himself up and stumble forward.

I saw it then. Flying toward us from one of the craggy peaks in the distance. At first it looked like a small plane and then it veered and circled the towers. It was unmistakably a very large, winged creature – a dragon. It was not one of the graceful, magnificent kind you see in movies. This one was hideous and bloated. It looked more like a flying komodo dragon with short stubby wings. Its torso was lizard-like and its fat legs dangled awkwardly. It didn't look like a creature that should even be able to fly, but there it was. I watched in horror as it started to bank and dive toward the poor man, who had fallen again and was trying to scoot himself along the ground.

Tyler yanked me down and clutched me tightly to his chest.

"We can't help him," he whispered in a tortured voice.

Deep inside I knew that it was true, but the man's screams tore me apart. I stifled my own cry and clutched Tyler tightly, praying for it to end. The sounds finally faded away and it was over – for now.

I was shaking uncontrollably and my leg had started to burn. It felt like it was on fire. I reached down to rub it and realized that it was hurting exactly where I had been shot with the poisonous arrow. I couldn't think about that now. I had to focus.

"Grayson drew this?" I could barely speak.

Tyler nodded.

"This is a nightmare." I managed to mumble, although my face felt frozen.

"Yeah. Something like that." Tyler's voice was heavy with fear and I was still shaking. This was way more than either of us had bargained for.

4 x 4 x 4

It was something my dad had taught me and I struggled to remember it now. To the count of four, it was four breaths in and four breaths out for four minutes. I forced myself to breathe in slowly for four counts and then exhale for four counts.

"We just have to breathe." I managed to say as I started the next cycle. Tyler followed my lead. For a few minutes we just sat there breathing in a rhythmic calming way.

Finally I was able to think in a halfway coherent manner – although my trembling had not stopped and my leg was still on fire. I pulled up the leg of my pants but it looked perfectly fine.

"When I was six, my dad was on leave and we went to the beach for vacation. We were in a hotel room watching some silly game show on TV. Everyone was laughing and having fun. It was one of the few happy times I remember with Mom and Dad and Mariela – she is my half-sister – all of us together. I fell asleep on the couch and when I woke up the room was dark and everyone was gone. They were only out by the pool, but I didn't know that. I thought they had left me. I couldn't hear them. The TV was still on, and there was this documentary about komodo dragons. I was terrified, but I was frozen to the couch -- afraid to get up and run. Those giant lizards looked like they were in the room with me. The narrator went on and on about how they bit their prey and then stalked it for days until it got so sick and weak from the poison they killed it. He told about a little village boy that had been bitten and tracked and finally killed. When I heard that I started screaming. Dad came and got me, but I couldn't stop screaming."

I stopped my story abruptly -- feeling stupid for blurting the whole thing out.

"That thing - it looked like a komodo dragon with wings." I ended lamely.

"Yeah, it did." The day had grown light while I was talking and I could see Tyler's face clearly. His jaw was clamped so tightly the muscles in his cheeks were flinching.

"Danni, I don't know how this whole princess - convergence thing works, but this may be more than we can handle. It's okay if you want to fall back and get more help or something."

"Are you asking me if I want to quit?"

"Yes, that's exactly what I'm asking. You don't have to do this. You should never have been put in this position."

I inched myself up to look over the top of the embankment again. In full morning light, the fortress looked remarkably benign - almost deserted -- but there was no telling what horrors were happening inside right now or how long we had before someone else was tossed out as dragon feed. I could see the barred window to Kyna's cell more clearly now. It was only about two stories off the ground. Surely we could get to her. We couldn't just leave her here.

I slid back down and looked at Tyler. I already knew by his expression that he was not going to abandon her either.

"We can do this," I said with newfound courage, realizing it was critical that we both believed that we could succeed. "I don't know how this whole princess thing works either, but I think we are here because we can do this. I'm all in. You?"

Tyler suddenly gave me a hotshot football hero grin. "Oh, I'm in." In the morning light, his clean-cut, all-American handsomeness was a little disarming and I tried not to think about how bedraggled I must look after all the walking, wind, and rain – oh, and the crawling in the dirt. I looked away quickly and felt my face go red, so I changed the subject.

"We need to get off this hill and find some cover. We are sitting ducks out here."

Tyler glanced around. "Not a lot of cover around."

"What about those rocks up ahead? Do you think they are the same ones in Grayson's painting?" Grayson had painted a barred window behind Kyna in her cell and I remembered the strange rock formation he had included in the view. There was a large mound of boulders not far from us.

We both edged up just enough to see the rocks.

"I think you're right," Tyler agreed. "They did have an unusual shape and so do those."

"Do you think they are significant?"

"I think everything Grayson drew was significant. Kyna was trying to show him how to find her."

"If we can get there, it looks like there are crevices we can hide in. There's a big hollow place on the right side."

"Yeah, I see it. Think we can make it? It's about twenty yards."

"Spoken like a football jock." I managed a smile and Tyler smiled back.

"We can make it." I said confidently as I pulled out my dagger and started cutting at some of the ivy-like vines on the bank. "I just hope this isn't poison ivy." I handed a piece to Tyler.

A few minutes later we were wrapped up in vines like a Christmas tree and rubbing dirt on our faces. We had grown quiet with the realization that we were about to move up and out into the open. Our eyes met and for a moment we just looked at one another. I had so much respect for Tyler even though he was looking pretty goofy right now with vines growing out of his head. I was sure that I looked equally silly.

"Some princess get-up, huh?" I tried to laugh but I could feel fear growing in my chest.

"You look beautiful." His response caught me off guard and I felt my face getting hot. I tried to joke it off.

"Thanks….uh…you too?" I tugged at one of his vine dreadlocks.

But we were too scared to be silly. We grew quiet again.

"You ready?" Tyler finally asked.

"Ready." I nodded and I crawled up and out into the field.

For the next several minutes we crept slowly and steadily through the scraggly brush in the field toward the rock formation with the hope that anyone in the fortress that might look our way would only see a slight wind moving through some weeds. We were getting close to the rocks when we heard it.

BONG.

BONG.

BONG...

The steady sound of the gong was coming from the top of one of turrets. We both froze in terror. I couldn't see the fortress entrance without lifting my head. Had they thrown another poor soul out to be a dragon meal or was it coming for us? Ever so slowly I moved my hand to the hilt of my dagger. I wasn't going down without a fight. I tried to imagine what my dad would do right now. I wasn't going to let myself even consider the unthinkable.

We heard the sound of its wings before it reached us...a heavy smash as their weight hit the air. I gripped my dagger tightly. I couldn't see Tyler, but I prayed that he had found a way to be ready, too. And then it soared over us – the size of a school bus – casting a huge shadow as it banked and headed toward the fortress. I could hear the screams as its victim was lifted into the air and carried away. I wanted to scream too, but I didn't. Instead I screamed in my mind.

WHY IS THIS HAPPENING?

"Danni." It was a soft whisper from Tyler. I didn't answer. I couldn't. Tears were streaming down my face, which was pressed to the dirt. I finally made myself move and slowly started to crawl toward the rocks again. Once there, I scrambled up into the cleft and wiped my eyes. Tyler squeezed in across from me. The crack was just big enough to accommodate us both and I felt gratitude for the momentary feeling of safety it provided. I could see that Tyler was unnerved, too. I had no clue what we were going to do next. Storm the castle? We had no idea what was waiting for us on the other side of those walls.

I shifted my weight and the rock I was leaning against broke loose and collapsed into a hole underneath the outcropping. Tyler quickly grabbed my legs or else I would have fallen in right behind it. The rock and a small landslide of gravel smashed loudly onto something below and then everything grew quiet. We froze in place, fearful that our hiding place had been exposed, but the stillness remained undisturbed. Tyler pulled the flashlight out of his tunic and leaned into the hole. A minute later he sat up and handed it to me.

"You gotta see this." We edged around each other so that I could lean into the hole. I was grateful for Tyler's strong grip on my waist. I flooded the area with light and experienced another one of those overwhelming moments that defy description.

"Wow."

The light revealed a glittering chamber that appeared to hewn out of solid diamond and gemstone walls. It wasn't a cave – it was clearly manmade – and it sparkled like a room full of mirror balls. There was a tunnel leading toward the fortress, too.

I struggled to sit up and Tyler pulled me out.

"Unbelievable." At least it sounded better than "wow."

"Did you see the tunnel?" Tyler asked.

"It looks like it heads straight to the fortress, doesn't it?" I nodded. "You know, a lot of old castles had escape tunnels, do you think that's what this is?"

"It could be. But where would they escape to? There's nothing out here but more fields."

"True. But at least they could run – they wouldn't be trapped if the castle was under siege. Or maybe it's for mounting a sneak attack from behind."

"Well, we've come this far," his eyes met mine. "Do you want to at least see where the tunnel takes us?"

I nodded. "There are people dying here. Maybe we can do something about that."

We didn't hesitate. Tyler took my hands and lowered me into the hole. There were makeshift stone steps which made getting down easy and would make getting back out easy, too. I was especially grateful for that.

CHAPTER 10

The tunnel was quite a work of art, hewn from layer upon layer of dazzling gemstones. Our bright flashlight had turned it into a radiant passageway, but even one small candle would have created plenty of light in this shimmering underpass.

We were able to move quickly and it wasn't long before I grabbed Tyler's arm to get him to stop.

"Do you hear that?"

It was music – ever so faint – but lilting music, almost like a waltz.

Tyler nodded. From this point on, we made a special effort not to make any noise, but it didn't seem to matter because the music was growing steadily louder as we made our way toward the fortress. It seemed to have a life of its own, swirling down the tunnel toward us and around us, and was quite appealing even if it did sound a bit other-worldly. I couldn't seem to place any of the instruments responsible for its ethereal melody.

We had to be directly under the fortress now. The music was coming from overhead, and the tunnel had opened up into another glittering chamber with half carved clumps of rock at one end that formed another makeshift stairway – only it ended at a solid rock wall. It looked like this escape route had been sealed off a long time ago.

Tyler yawned and his stomach growled simultaneously.

"I could use one of Sparkle-Butt's snacks right about now," he whispered.

I had to smile. For just a second I wondered what Abbey and Grayson were doing, and found myself yawning, too. The music was so soothing and we hadn't had any sleep. I was almost forgetting to be on high-alert and afraid.

Tyler sat down on one of the rock steps and leaned his head back against the glittering wall.

"What's next, Princess? Looks like a dead end."

I sat down next to his feet and leaned back, too. I was feeling so sleepy.

The flashlight suddenly fell out of Tyler's hand and smacked the floor, causing me to jump. One glance upward told me that Tyler had fallen asleep, his mouth hanging open in a slight snore.

I yawned again. In the back of mind it occurred to me that this was not a good thing for us to be doing right now.

"WAKE UP OR YOU WILL DIE!"

Pax's face was inches from mine and he was screaming at the top of his lungs. His silvery blue eyes were ablaze. It was enough to make me jerk and stand up immediately. I had fallen asleep – I couldn't tell for how long. The flashlight was still burning – but maybe not quite as brightly. I knew immediately that it was the music that had lulled me into a stupor. I felt drugged. I shook Tyler by the shoulders and he moaned a little bit, but I couldn't wake him. I had to think quickly. The music was still playing and it was incredibly sensual, coiling around my brain and flowing down into my body like an internal caress. I wanted so much to give into it. This must be what it feels like to do drugs, I thought. It was terrifying and euphoric all at the same time – beckoning me in such an inviting way to slip into sweet nothingness. Begging me to give in to the empty delight of it all.

I shook my head and stooped down to find two little rocks. I used my dagger and cut small pieces of material from my shirt, and fashioned earplugs by rolling the rocks up in the material. I started to put them into Tyler's ears, but then I remembered what the flight attendants all say about putting on your own oxygen mask first and then helping your neighbor. It made sense. If I collapsed and Tyler didn't wake up, we might be trapped in the music's spell forever. I felt a sense of relief the minute I placed the rocks in my ears.

I quickly did the same for Tyler and tried to shake him awake. After several attempts, I finally kicked him in the shin with all my might.

"What? Ow! Why did you do that?" he shouted.

I quickly clamped my hand over his mouth and pulled out one of his earplugs to whisper rapidly, "We've been drugged by the music – we were both asleep – I don't know how long," and I plugged his ear again. I hoped no one had heard us, but at least the music was very loud here.

It took a few minutes for everything to register, but Tyler finally nodded his understanding and pushed my hand away. He carefully pulled out one of the improvised earplugs and listened for a second, and then swiftly replaced it. I pointed to the top of the stairs we were sitting on. There had to be some kind of opening up there because that's where the music was coming from.

He nodded his agreement. We were going to have to communicate with hand signals from here on out. I scaled the stairs first with Tyler right behind. When we reached the top, we were only about twenty feet above the chamber. I didn't see it at first, but I felt the air coming from a fissure between the supporting wall and the barrier wall we were facing. We had to step out onto a small ledge to get to it, but if we could squeeze through, we might come out on the other side. I gave Tyler a questioning glance and he nodded. I just hoped there weren't any giant spiders in the opening or something even more horrible waiting for us on the other side.

The maneuver was surprisingly easy. I slid through first with Tyler right behind. We found ourselves standing in bright sunlight in a large rectangular courtyard surrounded on all sides by high rock walls that looked like they were on the verge of collapse. While the fortress had appeared to be sound from the outside, its interior was not much more than a ruin. Moss was growing everywhere and the ancient rock walls were crumbling. They rose up for three stories. Each level had open archways that looked down on the yard where we stood. Perhaps the walls had once sported balconies that had long since rotted away.

I felt exposed and quickly motioned to Tyler. We ran to the nearest archway on the ground level. I could hear the music more clearly now even through my prehistoric earplugs, but thankfully it didn't seem have the same stupefying effect as before. The sparkly rocks in our ears had to be subduing its influence. It was coming from the second floor, of that much I was sure.

As if reading each other's thoughts, we turned and carefully advanced into the cool, dark, musty interior of the fortress. All we found were more crumbling walls illuminated by hazy shafts of sunlight finding its way in through the cracks.

My mind was racing. Where had the prisoners come from? I could feel all the hairs on my neck stand on end. There was something very wrong with this place. I had a mental picture of people being lured here by the music and then kept in a sleeping state until they were tossed out as dragon food. I shuddered and

Tyler touched my arm to make sure I was all right. I nodded, although I really wasn't.

Tyler motioned to the corner of the room and I saw what he was looking at. There were a couple of small stone steps that seemed to disappear into the wall. As we got closer, we could see that they actually corkscrewed upward and out of sight. At the top we found ourselves in another chamber much like the one below. A large arched opening set into the fortress wall allowed more light in.

A movement in the corner caused both of us to freeze with shock. We weren't alone. It took a second to make out the little boy huddled in a crumbled out section of the wall. He was horribly pale and frail, and his eyes had a look that I had seen in history class when they showed pictures of child victims of war. His clothes were so filthy that I couldn't tell what they had originally looked like. He couldn't be much older than Abbey.

I immediately started toward him, but Tyler grabbed my arm.

"It could be a trap," he mouthed.

I knew he might be right and I stopped. Some of the seductive music was getting through and I struggled against its sensual tug at my brain. I wasn't thinking straight. I readjusted my earplugs. I needed to get us out of here alive and that required a clear head.

The little boy was just staring at us and I could tell by his expression that he wasn't sure if we were real or not. I wondered why the music wasn't having any effect on him. His eyes slowly moved from us to the archway that led to the next room. He was trying to tell us something. Just then a large dark shadow passed by the opening and I could see him start to shake with fear. Tyler and I immediately took a step backward just as the music stopped.

BONG.

The boy tried to push himself back further into the wall. There was a muffled noise of a struggle from the next room.

BONG.

I carefully raised my finger to my lips and the boy nodded jerkily as if he understood. I removed one of my earplugs and Tyler did the same.

BONG.

We could hear voices from the next room plainly now. It sounded like several people were waking up and questioning what was going on as their voices grew louder and louder and filled with anxiety.

BONG.

Someone started screaming and all the while the gong sounded steadily from somewhere above us.

BONG.

Something flying by the window obstructed the sunlight and for a moment the chamber plummeted into darkness.

BONG.

And then it was light again and we could hear screams from below.

The little boy was shaking violently. I felt my whole chest burn with rage.

Then just as suddenly as it had stopped, the music started again and the noise in the next room subsided. With one ear unplugged, I could feel the hypnotic effects of the melody almost immediately. Tyler had already put the cloth-covered rock back in his ear, but I needed to talk to the boy.

I carefully made my way toward him. As I passed the archway, I could see the people in the next room. They had already succumbed to the music. There was at least a dozen of them – some in chairs, some on the floor – some dressed in rags and some in finery. They seemed to be completely unguarded, but then, why would they need to be? They were prisoners of the music.

I moved quickly to the little boy and scooted into the nook with him. He had the look of a trapped wild animal and he smelled like one, too. I wondered how long he had been hiding in here. I put my arms around him. I tried not to let him see that I was really struggling to stay coherent – the music was so inviting – but looking down into his dark, terrified eyes gave me strength to resist it.

"What is your name?" I whispered, hoping he would understand. He seemed to.

"Grif."

"Grif, where are your parents? Your mom and dad?"

His eyes glazed for a second and then he lifted his hand and pointed to the open window. He blinked back tears as if he had already decided that crying was not going to help.

"Grif, you have to listen to me, okay? We need to find a girl – she's about my age – her name is Kyna. Do you know where she is? Have you seen her?" I had to shake my head sharply to fight off the lethargy that was trying to overtake my mind and body.

Grif nodded slowly and pointed upward. Tyler had been watching us from across the room and I saw him glance around for another staircase, but there didn't seem to be one in this room.

I put my face close to Grif's in an effort to stay focused. I really needed to put the earplug back in.

"The music doesn't make you sleepy, does it?"

He shook his head.

"I need to block out the sound so I don't fall asleep. I'm going to put this back in my ear," I held up my homemade earplug, "and then my friend and I are going to go get that girl." I felt him start to wiggle in protest. "I want you stay here. We'll come back for you, okay?"

He shook his head in distress. "That's what they said." There was so much terror in his voice that I had to think of something fast. I looked at Tyler and I could see his concern, but we both knew that taking the boy with us would be too much of a distraction. He was much safer here.

"Grif, my name is Danielle. I am the Princess of Geilgess. I promise you that I will come back for you. I won't leave you here. You are going home with me, okay?" I prayed inwardly that this was a promise I could keep, but I knew for sure that I had no intention of leaving this place without him.

My words seemed to have the desired effect and he nodded. I was actually starting to feel dizzy, so I gave him a squeeze.

"Stay right here and be ready, okay? We'll be back soon and we may have to move really fast." He nodded again and I saw a renewed courage in his little face. It made me want to cry, but I knew that getting emotional right now would only endanger all of us. I also had to keep fighting the part of me that wanted to just give up and go to sleep. My body felt like it weighed a thousand pounds.

"Grif, do you know where the stairs are?" He nodded again and pointed toward the room with all the sleeping people.

I was going to have to put the earplug back in immediately or all would be lost. I wondered why the music did not make Grif sleepy. Maybe it was because of his age or his innocence. I leaned in close to be sure that he could hear me.

"I will be back for you…" I said, "…I promise." It was a relief to put the rock back in my ear and buffer the hypnotic strains of the music, but it took a few minutes for me to regain my strength. Tyler had remained on alert at the other side of the room. I motioned toward the archway to the next room and then I motioned upward. He understood. I squeezed Grif's hand and crawled out of the hole. I was feeling a strange sense of urgency now. We needed to find Kyna and get out of here fast.

The walk through the chamber of sleeping people was surreal. They had fallen asleep even in the middle of their despair – enticed by the strangely inviting notes of a death melody. One woman dressed in an elegant velvet chemise still had tears on her cheeks as she smiled in her sleep – comforted by its evil spell. I thought of Pax and wondered if he had ever moved in and out of these people's heads in his search for Kyna. My mind was screaming that I needed to help them all, but I didn't know how. I prayed that something would come to me.

The next chamber was smaller and square. It only contained a crumbling rock stairwell that went both up and down. It was distinctively darker and cooler than the previous rooms, with only one small slit of a window in the side of the wall above us to let in the light. I instinctively knew that this was the prison tower. There was a landing and a door at the top of the stairs. My pulse quickened. If Kyna was up there, it was up to us to save her.

I had to force my legs to move. The realization that someone or something had dragged the last victim out of the next room and fed it to a dragon was immobilizing. Whatever had done that couldn't be far away. As we climbed, Tyler kept scanning the area above and below us. I wished that we could talk but we were saying volumes with our eyes. Right now I hoped that he could read in my face how grateful I was that he was here with me.

About halfway to the landing, one of the steps broke off and my foot slipped, sending a spray of rocks to the floor below. Tyler reached out to steady me with a hand at my waist. He was so strong – all that weight-lifting and football practice had given him an incredible body. Our eyes met as I mouthed a "thank you" to him. His face was deadly serious, but for a split-second I saw a touch of mischief twitch around his lips. If we had been in a different circumstance, he would probably have given me a hard time about my lack of coordination or propensity for falling and fainting. I almost smiled but forced myself to turn away and keep moving upward.

We made it to the top without further incident, but the landing was small and unstable and the large stone slab wobbled as if it might break free at any moment. There was nothing to hold on to so we had to balance as best we could. We could go no further…we had come face to face with a large wooden door set into a rock archway. The wood was dark and plain with the exception of two rows of metal studs that gave it a definitive look of a prison door. The handle was a round, rusted metal ring with a lock and keyhole that looked like it had not been used in years.

Could Kyna really be inside? There was only one way to find out. For several minutes we tried in vain to get the door to open, all the while keeping watch below us. My head was starting to throb from the endless dull drone of the music. I took out my dagger and tried to pry open the lock. The hinges were recessed behind the stone of the archway so removing them was not an option. This was taking way too long and I was starting to feel tremendous anxiety. My mind kept going back to the drugged people in the room below, and to little Grif huddled in the corner of a wall. This had to work. There had to be some way to get into the room.

"Danni!"

Tyler had been trying to get my attention. He motioned with his eyes toward my chest. For a moment I didn't understand and then slow realization spread through me. The key. As I grasped the necklace my dad gave me so many years ago, I flashed back to Queen Avezdenia reaching out to touch it before she left us after our meeting at Geilgess. Could it really be this key that would open the cell door?

I carefully took the necklace off and pressed it into the lock. It turned with a heavy click. I looked at Tyler in disbelief, and I could see that he was just as amazed as I was. I quickly put the key back around my neck. Every fiber of my being was telling me that we were running out of time. I would have to think about this later…the implications were too overwhelming to even consider right now. I nodded to Tyler and we both pushed. The heavy door grated along the floor as it opened.

This room was different from the rest. Instead of rough rocks for a floor, this one had wooden slats. Nasty old tapestries were hanging from the walls, and there was even a rotting wooden table in the center of the room and the remnants of an old, unused fireplace in one wall. It struck me that it had once been a prison cell for someone of importance.

I instantly recognized the barred, arched window across the room and went running over to look out of it. It was exactly as Grayson had painted it. There in the distance was the rock formation where we had been hiding only a little while ago.

It was Tyler who found Kyna lying next to the wall, partially hidden by one of the wall-coverings. Even in her sleep and as pale and emaciated as she was, she was stunningly beautiful. She was so still that for a moment I thought we were too late, but Tyler felt for her pulse and nodded. We quickly figured out that she was chained to the wall, just like in Grayson's picture. Tyler went to work to free her. He was able to pull the metal bolt out of the disintegrating rock and I helped him slide her tiny delicate foot out of the clamp. I quickly picked up two of the small rock fragments and fashioned earplugs for her with some more cloth from my shirt. As an afterthought, I stuffed a whole handful of rocks into my pocket while I was at it. I might not be able to put cloth around them, but they should still work on the people downstairs.

I was grateful for Tyler's strength. He lifted Kyna as though she didn't weigh anything, and seemed to be able to manage her and the bow and arrows with ease – but getting down the crumbling staircase wasn't going to be easy. I backed down ahead of him trying to help him find his footing. It was slow going, but we finally made it to the second floor level. Tyler stopped to rest. There was another set of stairs that continued downward to the ground floor, and they seemed to be much more solid.

I made an impulsive decision but I knew it was the right one. I leaned over and pulled out Tyler's earplug. I saw the music hit him full force like a drug as I leaned close to the side of his head.

"You have to keep going down, Tyler. Once you get to the ground level, all you have to do is cross the courtyard and you'll be at the gap in the wall and the entrance to the tunnel." I saw confusion all over his face as he tried to comprehend what I was saying and fight the effects of the music at the same time.

"I'm going to try and help those people." I pointed to the next room. "I'm going to put rocks in their ears – it may at least give them a fighting chance. Then I'm going to get the boy and I'll be right behind you."

Tyler started shaking his head.

"No way. I'll wait here. I'm not leaving you."

"You have to." I was surprised at the commanding tone of my voice. "We are running out of time." Of that I was certain. Even the air around us felt heavy with expectancy. The dragon feedings seemed to take place about an hour apart. Whatever controlled it was going to be coming for someone soon. We could not be here.

"We have to split up. It's going to take you longer to carry her. I will get this done and follow you. Just get to the rocks at the end of the tunnel. We'll be right behind you." I could see the agony of indecision on Tyler's face, but I could also see that he knew I was right. Kyna stirred briefly in his arms. It might take a while but she was going to regain consciousness.

"Remember," I struggled with my next words. "If anything...happens...she is royalty. She can get you home."

Tyler's jaw clenched tight, as he tried to control his emotions. "I'm not leaving here without you."

I tried to force a grateful smile but my lips were twitching with fear.

"Then we'd both better hurry. I'll see you in a few minutes." I placed the rock back in his ear and on impulse started to kiss his cheek, but he turned his head at the same moment and our lips brushed. I almost wanted to linger there, but I quickly pulled away and walked toward the archway that led to the next room. I turned to look back as Tyler hoisted Kyna again and started down the stairs. Our eyes met and I nodded at him, trying to let him know that he was doing the right thing.

I turned hurriedly and made my way into the chamber of sleeping people. It was terrifying to be alone with them and move among them as they lay there in a suspended state. I made myself focus on the task at hand. I counted fourteen people, most of them men. Judging by their clothes, some of them were miners or farmhands – they still had tools attached to leather belts around their middles. A few were very well dressed. I tried to fathom how they had come to be here. Perhaps they had been lured by rumors of diamonds like the sparkling ones in the tunnel. I couldn't wait around to find out.

I worked as quickly as I could, sorting through the stones and finding ones that would be big enough to block out the bewitching music but small enough to stay in. I could only hope they would wake up in time to defend themselves. There was nothing more I could do. I had to get to Grif, and I prayed that he had stayed put in his little hiding place in the next room.

He had. I found him still huddled in the wall space. From the stunned and grateful look on his face, I don't think he had really expected me to return. He was weak and stiff and I had to help him stand up.

"Are you ready?" I asked without removing my earplugs. I already knew that he wasn't much for talking. He nodded and took my hand with both of his as we made our way to the skinny spiral staircase in the corner. Within minutes we were on the ground floor and perched under an archway at the edge of the open yard. I was relieved that there was no sign of Tyler and Kyna. They had made it into the tunnel. We just had to catch up to them. I pointed out the crack in the wall to Grif and he nodded. I could see that he understood. He was a very smart little boy.

We were just starting to make a run for it when the music stopped. I didn't notice until I felt Grif pulling frantically on my hand. One look at his terrified face made me realize that its sinuous strains were no longer trying to worm their way into my head. I quickly pulled one of the plugs out and listened carefully. There was no gong clanging yet, but something had changed. The air was so oppressive it was difficult to breath.

And then I saw him.

He came striding from the shadows of one of the archways at the side of the courtyard, and he was dazzling. He was dressed in striking dark leathers from head to foot, and he wore a cape that capped his shoulders in a military fashion and trailed behind him for several feet. The cape shimmered in dirty rainbow colors as it slithered along the ground. It was made of dragon skin.

His streaked blonde hair was wildly and perfectly coiffed – he looked like the lead singer in an eighties rock band complete with a lot of dark eye shadow. He didn't bother to look at us but strode pointedly to the center of the courtyard and stood staring at the fracture in the rock wall that opened into the tunnel. I felt Grif cower behind me and grip my leg. I reached for the handle of my dagger.

"I believe you took something that belongs to me." His voice was almost sensuous. He cocked his head slightly to look at me and surprised me with a smile.

"And who might you be?" He asked in a supremely condescending way as he sidled a few steps toward us. I nudged Grif with my leg and we took a few steps back. I did not feel the need to respond. The smile faded and his face grew hard with annoyance at my silence, as if he were hoping to toy with me a bit more before feeding me to his dragon pet.

"I really must have her back, you see. She is promised." His voice had taken a malevolent tone to let me know that his tolerance was at an end. A thousand thoughts were trying to take charge in my brain all at once as I considered our options. It was my dad's voice that pierced through all the chatter.

"Don't stay engaged if you can escape. Find your opening and run." He was right. There was no way this guy was going to let us past him into the tunnel. We were going to have to retreat and make a run for it.

"She doesn't belong to you." I said flatly, without emotion. I wasn't going to give him the pleasure of sounding afraid.

I could see his face grow red with anger. He let out

a massive growl that actually caused some of the loose rocks to crumble down the side of the ruins around us.

"Then I'll need something else to trade." He barked and pointed a finger at me. When he did the entire atmosphere exploded around us with the sounds of a thousand musical instruments all screeching in horrible dissonance. I grabbed my ears and managed to get the earplug back in. Thankfully, Grif didn't seem to hear it. I knew the sound onslaught was meant to immobilize me, but thanks to the earplugs, it gave us our moment. I grabbed Grif's hand and we ran back into the fortress and out through the crumbling opening at the front that must have been its original gate. The stony ground went downhill sharply and I imagined that a drawbridge had once spanned the gully. We were going to have to climb down and then back up. It took me a minute to locate the big mound of rocks across the field that marked the entrance to the tunnel. They were much further away from this side of the castle. I prayed that Tyler and Kyna were almost there.

As we scrambled down the hill, I looked back and saw that the Dragon Prince – or whatever his name was – had followed us only as far as the entrance. He was just standing there with a cold, glittery smirk on his face.

With the first sound of the gong, I understood why.

BONG.

I grabbed Grif's hand and we scooted down the rest of the embankment and then crawled up the other side.

BONG.

Once we were back up to the level field I pointed to the rocks and yelled for him to run.

BONG.

I pulled out the earplugs and tossed them, trying to remember how many times the gong had sounded before the dragon had snatched its victims.

BONG.

I shouldn't have bothered. I glanced by over my shoulder just in time to see the dragon launch from the mountain behind the fortress.

BONG.

Grif stumbled and I helped him up. He was running as fast as he could but he was weak and slowing down. There was no way that we were going to make it to the outcropping in time.

BONG.

"Look!" To my surprise Grif spoke and pointed toward the rocks. I saw Tyler and Kyna emerging from below ground. She was awake, but leaning on him heavily. He helped her sit down on one of the rocks. It only took him only seconds to assess our situation. He quickly took a stance, nocked an arrow and took aim. I heard it whiz by over our heads, followed by a loud screech. Behind us the dragon dropped to ground with the arrow in its wing, but it kept coming.

I picked Grif up and started running again as Tyler's arrows continued to fly around us. I heard more screeching from behind, but I could also feel the ground vibrate as the dragon gained on us. It was wounded, but the arrows weren't doing enough damage to stop it. My arms and chest and legs were burning and I wasn't sure how much longer I could run with Grif in my arms.

The sky had quickly grown very dark and I was surprised to hear thunder and feel rain smacking my face. And then I saw her. Kyna was standing up by the mound of rocks with her arms outstretched.

She is summoning a convergence.

She was frail-looking and her clothes were in tatters, but no one would mistake her for anything but royalty as she stood there with the wind whipping her hair. In seconds a bright, shimmering tunnel appeared behind her – opening up a pathway to take us home.

Tyler had exhausted his arrows. He threw his bow down and ran to us, grabbing Grif from my arms. I could tell that the effort to create the convergence had drained what little energy Kyna had left and she was on the verge of collapse. Tyler threw his other arm around her to help her along and we all ran toward the bright tunnel.

But the dragon wasn't giving up. Tyler, Kyna, and Grif went into the convergence ahead of me. I had just stepped into the tunnel when I felt something sharp clamp down on my side. It was so excruciatingly painful that I couldn't even scream. To my horror the dragon was in the convergence with me – with us. I struggled to get free and managed to slash its nose with my dagger. My blow did some damage and it let go. I fell backwards and scrambled away on the ground, finally getting upright again, although the swirling wind and rain weren't helping.

I was having trouble getting my breath. I don't think Tyler was even aware of what had happened to me. He had his hands full trying to hold Grif and help Kyna. All I could do was limp along and clutch my side where the blood was seeping through my shredded shirt. I prayed that the convergence would end soon and that the Defenders would be waiting there to stop this horrible beast before it hurt anyone else. Glancing over my shoulder I could see the dragon only yards behind me. It was heavily wounded, but kept coming. It had bitten me – now all it had to do was wait for me to succumb to the poison.

The convergence ended abruptly with a massive bolt of lightning and clap of thunder. It simply disappeared and without warning we were running in the woods. This forest was laid out as though it was expecting an army to come through, and offered a wide passageway with large trees lining our course. It wasn't the Midnight Forest – and it wasn't the forest that had brought us to Geilgess. These woods were different – they seemed cultivated and well-groomed.

Geilgess must be surrounded on all sides by different forests that lead to other worlds, I thought, as I fought the urge to throw up.

I didn't know how much longer I could run when I saw a bright opening ahead that meant we were almost out of the woods. That hope gave me renewed strength and I managed to catch up with the others. We burst out into the field, but much to my dismay there were no Defenders in sight. Geilgess stood shining in the distance on its high hill, resplendent in the sunshine, but it was a side of the castle I had not seen. It dawned on me that the Defenders must be waiting at the entrance to the Midnight Forest where we left them. We had emerged in some other place.

Tyler turned to look at me and I saw the horror in his eyes. I knew the dragon must be right behind me. In a split second decision I purposely turned and ran in a different direction. I knew the dragon would follow me and leave them alone. There was nothing Tyler could do now anyway but save Grif and Kyna. He was smart enough to know that.

In the light of day as I looked back, I could see that one of the dragon's wings was dragging the ground, but it had no intention of giving me up. It had slowed down a little, but its tongue was flicking in and out to keep my scent and I could tell that it was ready to charge me again. I wasn't sure if I could run much further.

"Hit hard." I heard my dad's voice for the second time today. Strangely enough, I knew what it meant.

Dad used to say that in a combat situation there might only be the opportunity for one defensive blow and it had to count. "You have to find your opponent's most vulnerable area and hit it with all your might." A well-placed strike could render even a massive opponent totally helpless.

I knew that at some point I was going to have to turn around and make a stand against the dragon. I couldn't run much longer and there was no place to go but uphill toward the castle. I just didn't have the strength.

A large boulder was sticking out of the ground and into the side of a bank just ahead. I saw a maneuver in my mind's eye that might work. I only had a second to commit to it, and I did. I summoned all my strength and ran as hard as I could toward the big rock. I was going to run up it for height and leverage and then turn around and try to stab the dragon in the chest or throat. It was the only chance I had to survive.

Glancing back, I saw that the dragon had sensed my increase in speed and was starting to run faster too. That's okay, I thought. I was going to let its speed do some of my work. The only thing I had to do was find an unprotected spot and sink the blade in.

It seemed as though it happened in slow motion, but it was actually over in seconds. I ran up the rock, spun around, and went airborne just as the dragon was rearing up to take another bite. I used both hands to plunge the dagger into what I hoped was a lung and then rolled over its wing and onto the ground. I hit hard and tumbled down the slope to a stop. There was no more fight left in me. Either it had worked or the dragon would end me now. I could hear it flopping behind me, but I was unable to turn my head to see what it was doing.

As I lay there with the side of my face in the dirt, I could see Tyler running toward me. Kyna was on the ground, too, and little Grif was standing next to her. His face was pale with shock, but didn't seem to be hurt.

I was relieved to see that their little group was about to be overtaken by an army of riders. It was the Defenders galloping toward us at full speed. I could feel the ground vibrate with the power of so many running horses. The Defenders must have heard the thunder and seen the lightning from the convergence and realized they were waiting at the wrong place.

The riders split apart to avoid Tyler, Kyna, and Grif and then reconnected, blocking my view. I knew Arthmael was the lead, I recognized his distinctive helmet and armor. They thundered past me to finish off the dragon, which must have been trying to escape back to the forest. Tyler was running toward me again and there was one last horse galloping in my direction. Oddly, the rider wasn't wearing armor. He charged past Tyler and as he got closer I realized it was Grayson, looking perfectly majestic in the saddle with his palace vestments and his dark hair flying in the wind. I wondered where he had learned to ride a horse so well. And then it dawned on me that I would never find out. My burning wounds had turned into swollen numbness and that was probably a very bad thing. I was vaguely aware of Grayson throwing his leg over the horse and sliding to the ground before the horse even came to a stop.

He was running toward me with that worried frown on his forehead.

CHAPTER 11

The top step was cold against my back but I didn't mind so much. The view of the galaxy was spectacular. The two columns that had once supported the porch of the burned house now looked like pillars designed to support the glorious broad expanse of stars and planets overhead.

There was still that faint smell of soot in the air and I managed to turn my head sideways to look at the area where the house had once stood. I could almost imagine the rooms and the windows and the curtains, the fireplaces, and the pots and pans hanging in the kitchen.

All gone.

Past the backyard with the deserted swing set and the fields in the distance, I could just make out the faint light of dawn giving form to the horizon.

I wish Pax were here, I thought as I watched a star shoot across the sky.

"I'm here."

He was there. Sitting on the second step and holding my hand. I was very happy to see him and his softly glowing silver eyes. I tried to sit up but didn't have the strength, so I relaxed back onto the stone.

A tiny sparkly streak of light shimmered our way from the horizon.

"It's almost morning, isn't it?" I felt like there was so much that I was forgetting. It was unsettling. I clutched Pax's hand.

"Almost." He answered, and to my surprise, he kissed my hand and then reached over to stroke the hair from my forehead.

I was cold and I was starting to shake. I wished the sun would come up. I looked back toward the horizon and the light seem to be dancing just out of reach, teasing as if it were going to burst forth at any minute. An occasional glimmer would escape and trickle like water toward us but then it would pull back and hide again – as if it were playing a happy little game.

The thought made me want to smile, but my teeth were chattering.

"Something is wrong with me, isn't it?" I asked Pax. "I can't remember."

His expression didn't change but the glow in his eyes flickered.

"You've been wounded." He said in a tone that was even and unalarmed.

"Am I dying?" It was suddenly starting to make sense – this place.

"I think that is up to you." He stated calmly.

I wanted to thank him for being with me here like this, but the light from the horizon was suddenly very bright. The sun was about to make an appearance. I had to shield my eyes as I looked. To my astonishment I saw the silhouetted form of a man in the abandoned backyard. He was standing motionless near the old swing set. I couldn't see his face but I recognized his shape immediately.

"Dad!" I struggled to sit up.

"That's my dad," I turned to tell Pax, but he had vanished. I turned back just in time to see Dad walking away back toward the light. Everything grew a little darker with each step.

"Dad!" I screamed.

"Dad! Wait!" Why didn't he hear me?

Winnow was holding me tightly in her grip as I struggled to get down and go after Dad. "Please wait! Dad! Don't go!"

"There, there, now." Winnow tried to soothe. I was too weak to resist for long and I collapsed against her.

"There, now," she repeated. "The worst is over."

But it wasn't.

The pain was excruciating and unrelenting. I threw up until there was nothing left to throw up and then I threw up some more. In between bouts of retching, Winnow forced a ghastly green liquid down my throat. I alternated between shivering and sweating with poor Winnow sponging my forehead and trying to keep me covered up or cooled off.

I was hazily aware that I must be in the castle infirmary. It was a plain, small chamber although it did have the same arched ceilings as the other rooms in the castle. There were three empty beds along the wall and milky shafts of light drifting in through small barred windows.

I tried to ask about Tyler, Kyna, and Grif, but Winnow shushed me and said that everyone was fine and not to worry. I was going to throw up again, so I didn't argue. After I finished I was expecting her to have more of the green fluid waiting, but instead she stuck her finger in my mouth and rubbed some sickeningly sweet oil onto my gums. I tried to protest, but I immediately felt its effects. I sank back into the damp sheets and felt my whole body relax. I was falling, falling, falling backward and down into the place where dreams live.

I was going to a ball. That could be the only explanation for the immense dress I was wearing. It fluffed out around me in all directions like a soft blue waterfall. I wondered how many crinolines I was wearing to hold it up. The fitted satin bodice was cinched so tightly that my side was throbbing. I wondered if I might even be wearing glass slippers and giggled at the thought. When I tried to lift my skirts to see my feet I discovered that it was an impossibility, so I decided to just venture down the corridor I had found myself in.

I couldn't quite remember how I got here.

The high walls of the wide hallway were decorated with portraits of dour looking men and women and tapestries of gentry with their hounds preparing for a hunt. There was a dark unpleasantness about it that even the enormous brightly lit chandeliers and wall sconces couldn't dispel.

It was an unusually long corridor, but I could hear faint strains of music coming from somewhere up ahead. And sure enough I was soon approaching two very large doors with a footman waiting at each. They looked quite elegant in their white wigs and black velvet waistcoats lined with rows of impressive buttons.

The footmen bowed deeply as I approached and quickly opened the doors in unison. I was immediately engulfed by the sounds of music as it drifted up from somewhere below. I almost recognized the melody, but then it slipped my mind as I stepped through the doors and found myself at the top of an incredible staircase looking down at a sea of couples dancing in unison around an elegant ballroom. They were all dressed as beautifully as I was and no one seemed to notice me standing there.

I searched the crowd for anyone I knew and for a split second I thought I saw Mariela go dancing by, but after a few minutes of watching for her to show up again, I realized it was probably just someone with blonde hair like hers. There wasn't a handrail in sight, so I decided to make my way down the center of the massive staircase while everyone was still moving so no one would notice if I stumbled.

I was about halfway down when the music stopped. I glanced up from watching my step. The dancers had halted, too, and everyone in the ballroom was staring at me. I felt like I was back in the cafeteria on my first day of high school. With nothing to hold onto all I could do was try to finish the last few steps without falling flat on my face. I made it to the bottom and stopped awkwardly on the main floor.

No one moved. They all just kept staring at me like I was a party-crasher. I was just about to turn and flee back up the stairs when Jack Corbin emerged from the crowd.

"Wow." I think I said it out loud and felt my face grow hot. He was dressed from head-to-toe like Prince Charming, right down to the stripe on his tight pants and the military clusters on his shoulders. His hair had been smoothed back for the evening and when our eyes met, he broke into that gorgeous, charismatic smile that caused all the girls at school to swoon.

"You made it!" He took my hand and kissed it in true Prince Charming style. Obviously he was expecting me. Of course! This was a costume ball. That was it. I seemed to remember his family threw one last year. I must have been invited.

Before I could respond, he pulled me toward him until I was pressed tightly against his body. I thought he was going to kiss me again, but instead he took my other hand and the music immediately started up. Without warning we were dancing. I couldn't remember ever learning to waltz but I seemed to be doing okay – at least I wasn't stepping on his toes – and my voluminous skirts seem to float along nicely as well. All around us, the other couples were dancing again too, but they kept staring at us whenever they turned our way. I still didn't recognize anyone, but I tried to smile as they whirled past.

Something was wrong. I couldn't put my finger on it, but something wasn't quite right. When I was in eighth grade, I had gone to a dance and someone had spiked the punch. I felt like that now. Slightly intoxicated which was fun, but with the deep down feeling that it wasn't a good thing.

I'm just being silly, I told myself. I was at a wonderful party in a big house, dressed in a beautiful ball gown, and I was dancing with the most gorgeous guy at school. The music had slowed to a much more comfortable pace and I had the chance to look around. It was really a magnificent place – a palace really.

"Do you live here?" The minute I said it I realized how lame I sounded, and I tried to fix it. "It's beautiful."

Jack smiled down at me with that perfect face and I felt a little weak at the knees. "It belongs to the family. I'm glad you like it."

I had to look away because he was too close for comfort again. I tried to think of something else to say.

"How many rooms does it have?"

"Sixty-two, I think – something like that."

I wanted to ask exactly where it was located since I didn't remember getting here, but I decided it would be better to ask someone else later rather than to seem unsophisticated. Not only was Jack Corbin the most handsome guy at Commerce High, his family had to be incredibly wealthy to own all this. No wonder Mariela was upset when he kissed me.

Even though we had made several turns around the ballroom floor, I had still not seen the orchestra, or anyone else from school. All these people must be his parents' friends.

"Is Kim here?" That seemed like a safe question. I had to keep my head clear. He was holding me so close and breathing on my neck, which was making it really hard to think.

"Kim?"

There it was again. That strange little tickle in the pit of my stomach making me think that something wasn't quite right. Maybe he just didn't know Kim very well. They obviously moved in different circles.

"My friend from the mall."

"Oh, yes." His spoke right at my ear and I gave a little gasp. The vibration of his voice was enthralling. I actually sighed and I heard him chuckle but I didn't care.

"I could dance like this all night." Had I actually said that out loud? I was mortified for a second and then I heard him whisper, "Me, too," and I relaxed into him completely and put my head against his chest. We were like one person gliding perfectly around the dance floor. No one else mattered.

I kept trying to remember where I had heard the music before. It had such a strange, timeless feel to it. It could only belong in a splendid room like this. The ceiling was several stories high with an enormous glittering chandelier at its center. Beautiful brocade draperies cascaded down the walls and slender mirrors had been placed between the panels to add to the glow and sparkle as the dancers floated by. For just a second I thought I saw something strange as we waltzed by one of the mirrors, but Jack whirled me away in a different direction. I tilted my head back and allowed him to support me as I whirled around him. I laughed.

"Are you having fun, Princess?" He pulled me deliciously close until our lips were almost touching.

Did he call me "princess?"

There it was again. That tickle in the tummy. Kim would call it a gut-check. I smiled and hoped he couldn't tell.

"Oh, yes. Very much."

"Good," he chuckled as he pushed me away into a twirl. It was in the middle of the twirl that I saw our reflection in one of the mirrors on the wall. The boy who was spinning me around was not Jack Corbin, and he wasn't dressed like Prince Charming at all. I was dancing with the Dragon Prince, dressed in dark velvet, his blonde hair streaked and wild, his eyes rimmed in black.

Everything came flooding back to me at once and it was more than I could endure. The ruins, the dragon, the pain in my side. I staggered, but Prince Charming caught me and pulled me close. The expression on his face had changed. He seemed to be sniffing me with delight as if he could smell my fear. I struggled and managed to free myself from his grip only to trip over my skirt and go sprawling on the floor.

The music had stopped and so had all the dancers. They were just staring at me with unoccupied eyes. They were under a spell, just like the people at the fortress, only these people had not been used for dragon food – yet – they were merely his playthings – their souls had completely disappeared. This might have been Kyna's fate if we had not rescued her.

The pain in my side was almost unbearable. I tried to scoot away from him along the floor but kept getting caught in my dress. He still looked a little like Jack Corbin, but his *face was changing. One glance toward the mirrors revealed his true image.*

"Oh, please stop. This is so unbecoming of royalty." He seemed completely annoyed at this turn of events and rolled his eyes. He actually extended his hand to help me up which only made me scoot further away. He sighed.

"Have it your way, Princess." He reached down and grabbed me with a steel grip as he pulled me back to my feet and into his arms. My side felt like it was blistered as I struggled with all my might to push him away.

"You are a little spitfire, aren't you? I like that. Well, rats!" He actually made a comical face at me. "I was really looking forward to breaking you little…" he kissed my bare shoulder, "…by little." He kissed it again and then licked it as I tried to get out of his grip. "You might even have liked it." He suddenly shoved his face right into mine.

"Now it won't be so easy," he said cruelly.

I actually saw a look of surprise and even fear cross his face as I stopped struggling and glared back at him with deathly coldness.

"That's okay." My voice was like steel. "The only easy day was yesterday." It was something my dad used to say and the minute it left my mouth I found new courage. I had already made up my mind that I wasn't going to stay here and I sure wasn't going to die here.

I kicked him as hard as I could. He wasn't expecting it and bent over in pain. It gave me just enough time to get free of his grip. I escaped to the stairs. I was halfway up when I heard him laughing. I stopped to catch my breath and looked back at him. He was standing straight again, but he wasn't making any move to follow me.

"Good luck with that, Princess," he said, and as soon as he finished I heard the first strike of the clock.

BONG.

"You know what happens at midnight." He was so amused with himself that he applauded. He finished morphing into the full-on Dragon Prince right in front of my eyes.

BONG.

I knew it wasn't a clock. I knew exactly what it was.

BONG.

I started to run again to the sound of his maniacal laughter. Blood was seeping through the side of my pretty blue dress, but I made it to the top of the stairs clutching at the pain as if that would make it stop.

BONG.

I shoved past the footmen at the door who seemed unconcerned by my breakout. The hallway that stretched ahead of me seemed infinitely dark and long but I kept running.

BONG.

There had to be a door somewhere – a way out. If only I could remember how I got here.

BONG.

I needed a convergence. Kyna had done it. She had simply raised her arms and created a path between two worlds.

BONG.

If I were really a princess I should be able to do it, too. So far the convergences had found me, not the other way around.

BONG.

I stopped running and gasped for air. A thought went off in my mind like a light bulb. The question and the answer was as simple as whether or not I believed that I could be a princess.

BONG.

I looked back down the corridor. To my complete horror the shadow of a dragon was moving toward me along the wall. He was coming.

BONG.

There was no room for self-doubt. A kingdom was depending on me.

BONG.

I didn't even need to raise my arms.

CHAPTER 12

A brilliant flash of lightning illuminated the room as thunder shook the old castle to its core, and then the rain came. I could hear it pounding the stones in the courtyard below. It would make sense for the infirmary to be near the Defender's quarters - a place to help wounded warriors. A small fireplace at the far end of the room provided a warm, comforting glow. I was safe.

Winnow came in carrying a large iron pot. I watched her struggle to lift it onto a table and wished that I could help.

"Winnow?" My voice was weak but it came out. She practically flew to my side and leaned close with a mixture of relief and joy on her face.

"Princess!" She was busy feeling my forehead and cheeks.

"I didn't die." I managed. My throat was really sore - probably from all the vomiting.

She practically beamed even though I could see the exhaustion on her face.

"No you did not, Princess. Indeed, you did not."

"Thank you, Winnow." I weakly reached for her hand and she clasped mine in both of hers.

"Let's take a look then, shall we?" She lifted the thin little gown I was wearing and carefully removed the bandages from my side. I tried not to wince at the pain.

"Very good." She let out a little sigh of relief. She covered the wound back up and tucked the covers around me.

"Your body formed an abscess around the poison. We had to lance it to drain it. I don't think I've ever seen Arthmael that nervous before."

"Arthmael?"

"He's patched up many a warrior in his time, but I think you were his first Princess." She smiled and I could see a twinkle in her tired eyes.

I couldn't quite imagine Arthmael being nervous. I wanted to smile back at her but my mouth was too dry and my lips were sticking together. Winnow helped me sit up enough to take a sip of water.

"Better?" She asked and I nodded as she kindly sponged my face and neck with a cool cloth.

"Winnow, where is Pax?" I needed to make sure he was okay. He had been strangely absent from my recent nightmare – or maybe it wasn't a dream – I couldn't be sure of anything anymore. The lines of reality were so blurred now.

"Pax and Her Royal Highness, Kyna, were summoned to the Imperial Majesty's court as soon as she was strong enough to travel." Winnow spoke with a weighted voice and a cloud seemed to cross her face. "There are many decisions to be made now. It seems a dark time has found our little haven."

Her intonation made me shiver, and she immediately straightened up and changed the subject.

"You must get some rest now." She tucked the covers around me and paused to listen to the thunder rumble in the distance. The storm had moved on.

"It will be morning soon. Sleep now."

And I did. A deep, refreshing, dreamless sleep.

I awoke to the sound of swords clashing interspersed with laughter. It took me a moment to get my bearings. The infirmary was awash with bright morning light. I gingerly got out of bed, holding the bandages to my side. I felt a little dizzy at first but made my way over to the barred windows. The stone floor felt cool and solid underneath my feet.

I couldn't see anything but the empty courtyard below. Suddenly and to my delight, Grayson, Tyler, and Arthmael moved into view. Grayson and Tyler were wielding swords, and very slowly parrying under Arthmael's instruction.

Even though I didn't want to, I felt that tingly sensation when I looked at Grayson. He appeared right at home brandishing a sword. More than any of us he seemed to belong in this world. Both he and Tyler were dressed in loose muslin shirts with leather breastplates and arm guards for protection. I tried to remember what they had looked like before. The image of Grayson in his paint-splotched jeans and t-shirt, and Tyler in his shorts and sandals, seemed like something I dreamed a long time ago. I forced myself to think about Malvern and Granddad and my bedroom in LA. It was almost as if those lives belonged in a storybook I had read somewhere along the way.

A burst of giggles floated up and Abbey ran into view with Grif right on her heels. They were playing with sticks made to look like swords. I was pleased to see little Grif looking healthy. As if he sensed my thoughts, he stopped and looked up at my window. I waved but he couldn't see me, or if he did, he didn't wave back. After a second or two, they both ran out of sight again.

"Your Highness! Please! You shouldn't be out of bed." It was Winnow carrying a tray of what I hoped was breakfast. I was starved. She deposited the tray and managed a quick curtsy before hurrying over to escort me back to bed.

"I'm feeling much better, Winnow, really." However, I complied and allowed her to fuss over me.

"I'm glad to hear that, Princess, but you mustn't overdo. Here now. I thought you might like a bite of porridge."

Winnow's expression alternated between delight and dismay as I woofed down the delicious cereal without any ladylike manners.

"That was so good! Thank you, Winnow!" I decided it would be too much to ask for seconds so I scooted back down into the bed and watched her scurry around the room, laying out linens and putting things in order.

"How long have I been in here?" I asked. It had been a little surprising to see everyone outside as though nothing had happened.

"It's been six days now." Winnow answered and I could hear the fatigue in her voice.

"Six days!" It didn't seem possible.

"Her Royal Highness, Kyna, came to see you every day until she was called away. She very much wanted to meet you." The thought of the beautiful, pale Queen-to-be standing by my bedside while I was in a delirium made me blush.

"Have you heard anything from them?"

"No, but that is not unusual," Winnow sounded quite sure. "They were on their way to a meeting of the High Counsel. Many things must be decided." There was that phrase again.

I realized that they were probably trying to decide what to do with us. And now there was Grif.

"What will happen to Grif, Winnow? I couldn't leave him. His parents had been…." I stopped. I couldn't bring myself to say it. I felt a wave of anxiety wash over me at the memory of the fortress.

Winnow rushed to my side and smoothed the covers around me and plumped my pillow in an effort to comfort me.

"Of course you could not leave him, Princess. You did the right thing. Don't you fret about Grif. He and Lady Abigail are having a wonderful time. Those two are inseparable now."

"I can see that." I smiled, feeling a little relief knowing that Grif was going to be okay and that Abbey had someone her own age to play with.

"Grif is a special little boy," Winnow continued. "Arthmael says he will be a great Defender one day."

I suddenly felt very tired and stifled a yawn. Winnow pulled the coverlet up to my chin.

"Now it's time for you to rest, Your Highness." I wasn't going to argue.

I must have slept the day away because when I awoke it was dark outside again and Winnow was puttering near the fireplace – stirring something in a large pot that smelled wonderful.

"Winnow, don't you ever sleep? Why isn't there ever anyone to help you?" I startled her, but she rushed over to check on me, not forgetting her usual curtsy. I knew she would be offended if I asked her to stop so I didn't bother, although the curtsying still made me uncomfortable.

"I don't need any help, Your Highness. I can manage quite nicely."

"Well, I won't argue with that," I smiled. "You are wonderful, Winnow, but you must be tired."

"Not at all, Princess. Now how about a nice bowl of soup?"

"If that is what smells so good, I'll have two!" I laughed. I really was ravenous. I could tell that Winnow was pleased when I polished off the second bowl and thanked her.

"When can I see the others?" I was ready to get out of this room.

"I was thinking that perhaps tomorrow if you are feeling up to it. They've been asking to see you, too"

"Oh yes! I'm really feeling much better, Winnow – thanks to you."

"Well, we'll see how you feel in the morning, but for now you need to get some rest." There was no disagreeing with Winnow so I didn't try. I fell asleep happily thinking about seeing Grayson the next day.

To my surprise I awoke in the Princess Bedroom. It was beautifully bathed in morning light and all the strands of gold in the canopy drapes around the bed shimmered magically along with the gemstones in the swan's crown on the tapestry across the room. They sprayed a rainbow of color across the floor. I wasn't surprised to see Winnow fussing about near the dressing table. No matter where I was she always seemed to be just a breath away.

"How did I get here?" I asked in amazement as I sat up. I had somehow been transported to the other side of the castle.

Winnow turned and curtsied with a smile and then approached. "Arthmael stopped by to check on you last night and we decided that you would mend more quickly in your own room." I couldn't believe I had slept so soundly that being carried across the castle did not wake me up.

"I have to remember to thank him," I said as I slid out of bed gingerly. "He is my knight in shining armor – literally."

Winnow smiled in her all-knowing way. "He'll be happy to hear that, I'm sure. Now let's have a look at that wound and then we'll see what we can do about all *this*," she gave a little wave of her hand to indicate that the rest of my appearance needed some work, too.

An hour and half later I had been fed, bathed, bandaged, and my hair was laden with ribbons and pearls. What Winnow referred to as a "simple day dress" was prettier than any prom dress I had ever seen. It was a lovely soft shade of dusty rose with a slightly off the shoulder neckline. The bodice fit to the waist like a glove. From there, the skirt gently flared downward with a beautifully embroidered panel set into the front. Of course, the back had the obligatory train but it wasn't as long as the one I wore on the first evening. The sleeves were exquisite, too. They were fitted to just above the elbow and then the back of the sleeve gracefully cascaded halfway to the floor, revealing material inside that matched the pretty panel on the front of the dress. The lines were graceful and elegant, but there was nothing simple about this gown. It was altogether lovely and regal. Winnow had worked her magic once again.

"Are you sure you are not my fairy godmother?" I fluffed out the skirt and studied myself in the mirror. "This is so pretty, Winnow. You don't think it's too much for daytime?"

"You are a Princess now and must dress like one." Winnow chided, but to my surprise she produced the key my dad had given me, still on its ribbon, and fastened it around my neck.

"I thought you might like to wear this though." She looked very pleased with herself.

"Oh, Winnow! I thought it was lost. Thank you!" I couldn't resist hugging her which both pleased and embarrassed her.

She immediately busied herself by straightening up the dressing table.

"The others will meet you in the sitting room. They have been moved to more appropriate quarters for sleeping."

"Oh." I couldn't stop the disappointment that came out in my voice. I didn't like the idea of being the only person in this huge suite of rooms. It had been comforting to know that Grayson and Tyler were only a few doors away.

"Not to worry." Winnow had picked up on my concern. "They are close by. Besides, I think Master Grayson was going to get a permanent crick if he had to spend one more night in the maid's bed." She laughed and I tried to laugh, too.

"Now then. I am off to see to the meal if you'd like to go in, Your Highness."

"Thank you, Winnow. For everything." I added, because she really did seem like my fairy godmother. She curtsied and exited through the small service door. I turned and stood for just a moment, allowing myself to soak in the beauty of my enchanted bedroom. It was hard to explain but I felt like I belonged here now.

Castle Geilgess feels like home.

That thought was both comforting and disturbing. I quickly made my way down the corridor and past the two now empty maids' rooms. The sitting room was full of light flowing in from the balcony. Everything was the same – the exquisite tapestries and velvet chairs – even Abbey's castle dollhouse was still in its little niche. I realized I was nervous about seeing everyone, especially Grayson. I had a flashback of him sliding off the horse and running toward me as I lay on the ground. Just the thought of that day made me anxious.

Abbey and Grif arrived first. To my surprise they were accompanied by a young woman dressed in a long white uniform topped with a matching apron. Her hair was pulled back and tucked into a dainty white cap. Her plain attire couldn't hide the fact that she was very pretty. I started to say hello, but she curtsied and quickly left the room.

"Danni!" Abbey came running toward me but then stopped a few feet shy of my chair and did a little curtsy. She had on a puffy lavender dress and looked absolutely adorable.

"Don't I get a hug?" I stretched out my arms but she hesitated.

"Isa says that we are supposed to mind our manners."

"Was that Isa that came in with you?"

Abbey nodded. "She's our babysitter."

"Do you like her?"

Abbey nodded enthusiastically. "She's nice."

"Well, if she asks, you can tell Isa that I commanded you to give me a hug!" Abbey burst into giggles and ran to me. I squeezed her tight. Grif was still standing near the door and my heart cramped to see those large dark eyes again.

"Hi Grif. It's good to see you." I reached a hand out to him, but he didn't move forward. I could only imagine what must be going through his mind and how just seeing me must bring back all kinds of horrific memories. I had to think of something quick.

"I hear Arthmael is teaching you how to sword-fight!"

It wasn't exactly true but it worked. Grif's face brightened and he nodded excitedly.

"I hear you are very good. He thinks you will be a Defender someday."

Grif nodded again, and to my amazement he actually smiled and took a few steps forward. I thought he was going to say something, but Abbey interrupted.

"But Grif is going to come with us when we go home, right?" Abbey's question took me by surprise.

Thankfully I didn't have to reply because Abbey spied her dollhouse and went tearing across the room, squealing for Grif to follow her. Within minutes they were deep into a make-believe battle for the maid in the tower.

I was starting to feel anxious again. For all that had happened, I still had no idea what was going on. Not even one answer. I walked over to the balcony, and took a deep breath. The view of Geilgess was so picturesque that it belonged on a post card. The lake shimmered in the mid-morning sun, a group of swans were bobbing gracefully on its surface. And now that I knew what to look for, I could make out houses on the far side of the lake. The mountains in the distance created the perfect mystical, magical backdrop for this peaceful little kingdom.

"Winnow! I have no idea how to do this!" Tyler's voice caused me to whirl around. I had to put my hand over my mouth to keep from laughing out loud. He had burst into the room while trying to fasten the ties on the front of his fancy tunic. There were several decorative leather straps that were meant to run at a diagonal and tie near the neck on one side and he was having no luck with them. He looked very dashing in embroidered green velvet.

"Do you know where Winnow is?" He asked Abbey and Grif but they were too engrossed in their make-believe to pay him any attention.

"Can I help?" I stepped in from the balcony and startled him.

"Danni!" He rushed to me and before I knew what was happening, he picked me up and whirled me around. I managed a little "ouch" and he immediately put me down.

"Oh, I'm so sorry. Did I hurt you?"

"No. It's fine. I'm fine." He grabbed me and pulled me into his arms for a hug. I rested my head on his shoulder for a moment. It struck me that I fit just perfectly under his chin. He stepped back a little to look down at me and then pulled me close again for another hug.

"I thought I'd lost you." He whispered into my hair, then he stepped back so that he could look at me again. His face was in anguish. "Danni, I didn't know what was happening. I should have done something."

"Tyler, there was absolutely nothing you could have done except what you did. You had your hands full with Grif and Kyna." I hugged him tightly and then tilted my head back to look into his eyes to make sure he understood that it wasn't his fault. "I still can't believe you went with me in the first place. None of us would have made it out without you."

That seemed to help his feelings and his expression softened a little. Our faces were close and for a moment he gazed down into my eyes with such a strange look that I thought he might actually kiss me. To my surprise, I realized that I wanted him to, but he stepped back and pulled at the straps on his tunic.

"So, do you think you can help me with these? Who dresses like this anyway?" We both laughed, and laughing felt good.

"Don't let Winnow hear you say that."

"I know. I've already had one lecture today."

"Me, too!" I exclaimed as I finished the last tie-off for him. "She's pretty wonderful though."

"She's incredible."

I stepped back to admire my handiwork.

"You, sir, look very handsome and castle-appropriate."

Tyler smiled.

"You, Princess, look beautiful."

I know that my face must have turned beet red. I had to change the subject.

"So, where's Grayson?" A pained look flickered across Tyler's face, and I immediately wished that I hadn't asked.

"He's helping Winnow with a project, I think. He said if he didn't make it for lunch to let you know he would check on you later."

My heart sank a little. Here I was looking all princess-ey and he wasn't even going to be around.

"So how are you feeling? Really." Tyler escorted me to a divan and I sat down gratefully. He sat in a chair across from me but leaned forward to study my face.

"You're sure you are okay?"

I nodded. "I'm still a little sore, but I'm okay."

"I gotta tell you – that was one awesome move you made. It was unbelievable! You went completely airborne. You definitely have to join the cheer squad when we get home."

Our eyes met. I could tell that we were both thinking the same thing.

Are we ever going home?

"What do you think is going to happen now?" I asked, being careful to lower my voice so that Abbey and Grif couldn't hear, although they were totally focused on their little adventure. "I think Abbey needs to go home soon. She's lost some of her...sparkle."

"I know." Tyler nodded. "She's been talking about her father a lot. She has Grayson, but I think she needs her dad right now, too, and the security of her own home."

"I wonder what is happening back there. Do you think our faces are on milk cartons? Or maybe they don't even know we are gone."

Tyler shook his head. "I've been asking a lot of questions and trying to get answers, but everyone is so vague."

"Including our dear Winnow." I nodded.

"Especially our dear Winnow," Tyler said as he reached into his pocket and pulled out a folded up piece of paper. When he opened it, I saw that it had been torn from Grayson's little sketch book that he had presented to Queen Avazdenia.

"Do you remember seeing this?" He asked as he handed it to me. I did, but it didn't mean anything. It was just a blob with curving lines running through it.

"This is one of the first things that Grayson drew repeatedly. He would sit and draw this outline in class and then fill it in with little doodles – or I thought they were doodles until a couple of days ago. I found this same outline on a wall in the armory. It's a map of the realm."

I studied Grayson's blob again and saw how it could be the beginnings of a map.

"Seven kingdoms?" I asked. The boundaries were not well defined.

"From what Arthmael told me, there are six kingdoms. This seventh area," he pointed to the center area of the map, "is the capital. That is where the Queen resides. She is known as the Imperial Majesty, the High Queen, and the Regent of the Realm – so essentially she is in charge of everything. That's where Pax and Kyna are now."

"So, three princesses and three princes rule the kingdoms?"

Tyler shook his head. "No, these larger areas – I think this one is called Theyden Phayre and this one is where Kyna was going when she was abducted, Ferrinwold – these two are ruled by a king *and* a queen."

"So Kyna was going to be married?" I felt the blood drain from my face. I don't know why it surprised me. Royal marriages had been arranged all down through the ages.

"I think so."

"The Burdens of Queenhood." I stated flatly and Tyler tilted his head in a questioning way.

"Hmmm?"

"That's what she called it – the Queen, I mean – that's what she called it at our meeting." I explained.

"Oh, yeah." Tyler frowned and thought about it for a moment.

"Here's the weird thing," he continued. "When I was a scout, I had to create a survey map for one of my badges and I studied a lot of maps of the areas around Malvern. I didn't recognize it from Grayson's drawings at the time, but when I saw it on the wall in the armory and put two and two together – well, it's a really close match to the map I saw of the woods behind your grandfather's house – at least the outline is the same, but on a much smaller scale, of course."

"None of this makes sense, Tyler. So are we really just in the woods out back? Is it some kind of world within a world?"

"Or a gateway to another world maybe? I don't know." He shook his head, as befuddled as I was.

Or a real life enchanted forest.

I shivered unexpectedly and Tyler noticed.

"Tyler, did you see the guy at the fortress? The Dragon Prince?" It was a stupid name but it was the only thing I could think to call the person I had seen there.

"What!?" Tyler sat straight up as shock registered on his face. "No. I didn't see anyone. I assumed that someone was there to call the dragons, but...you saw someone?"

I nodded. "He blocked our way into the tunnel. That's why Grif and I came running out the front."

"Was he alone?"

"As far as I could tell. He was....creepy. He was all rocker-dark-side-rogue. He was controlling the music."

Tyler was quiet for a few minutes, trying to digest this latest bit of information.

"I just wish we had some answers," I continued."I hate feeling helpless like this." I was shivering again even though it was a warm morning.

Tyler moved over to sit next to me on the divan and took my hand. "Maybe we'll have some soon. Winnow said that Pax and Kyna have gone to a meeting of the High Counsel."

"She told me that, too. She also said dark times have found Geilgess, Tyler. I don't know what she meant but it can't be good." Tyler put his arm around me and I rested my head on his shoulder for a few minutes. It was strange that only a few days ago we were complete strangers and now we could sit in comfortable silence and watch Grif and Abbey play. I turned to look at the balcony with its radiant sunny view of the kingdom below and then I turned back to Tyler.

"I love this place, Tyler. I don't want anything bad to happen to it."

"Spoken like the true Princess of Geilgess," he said and he lightly kissed my forehead. I put my head back on his shoulder. It felt good and solid and safe, but I was suddenly very tired.

"Do you think it would be okay if I passed on lunch? I'd like to lie down for a little bit."

"Of course! You need to take it slow." Tyler popped up and helped me to my feet. "Allow me to escort you to your room, Your Royalness!" He extended his arm in a gallant manner and I took it. I turned to Abbey and Grif.

"Hey guys, I'm feeling a little tired so I'm going to rest for a while. I'll see you later, okay?"

"Ooh, don't go." Abbey whined. Grif just stood quietly watching me.

"I'm sorry, Abbey, but my side is hurting."

"Can we see where the dragon bit you?" Abbey asked with wide curious eyes. Grif quickly stepped backward at her suggestion.

"Maybe later. I'm all bandaged up right now. But I promise to show it to you." I gave Abbey a kiss on the top of her head and on a whim I stepped over and kissed Grif's head, too. To my surprise, he threw his arms around my skirt and hugged my legs. I squatted down to his level even though it made my side sting. I stroked his sweet face and smiled.

"You and I, Grif, we are going to be just fine. Okay?"

He nodded, and I wondered what was really going on behind those huge dark eyes of his. Tyler had to help me stand back up.

"I'll see you in a little while." I called back over my shoulder as we headed for the hallway.

"So, do you have a nice room now?" I asked Tyler as we walked past the empty maid's bedrooms.

"Yeah. It's very nice." He reached to open my bedroom door and let out a whistle as he saw the interior. "We got an upgrade for sure, but…wow!"

I laughed. I was glad to learn that I wasn't the only one with a limited vocabulary.

"It is pretty spectacular, isn't it?" I asked as we stood on the threshold of my princess bedroom cathedral. Tyler turned to me with a serious look on his face.

"You deserve it, Danni, and more. Get some rest, okay?" He squeezed my hand. "I'll see you tonight." I nodded and watched him walk back down the hall before I closed the door. I felt bad about spoiling lunch, but I was desperately tired and my side ached. I thought about trying to take off the dress, but I didn't have the energy to accomplish it without Winnow's help, so I very carefully climbed into bed, making every effort not to wrinkle it. The soft pillows felt wonderful.

CHAPTER 13

Lips were touching mine. Warm, gentle, searching. So nice. I opened my eyes slowly and it took me a moment to realize where I was. The princess bedroom was bathed in late afternoon light and Grayson was standing near my bed looking every bit the crown prince in a tunic done in rich teal velvet and accented with lavish golden embroidery. His long dark hair fell carelessly around his striking face, which sported the ever-present furrowed brow.

Had he kissed me or was I dreaming?

"Grayson?" I pushed up on my elbows and tried to blink away the sleepy cobwebs from my brain.

"Hey Danni. I wasn't sure if I should wake you. Winnow wanted me to check on you and see if you wanted to come downstairs for dinner. You didn't hear me knock. I was worried. Are you feeling okay?"

Of course he hadn't kissed me. How silly could I be!

I nodded, sitting all the way up, suddenly very self-conscious of how I must look. I only hoped that I wasn't drooling in my sleep.

"Yes. I'm good. Thank you. I'd love to go downstairs."

"I'll wait in the sitting room and walk down with you." Grayson turned quickly and left the room. Still a man of few words, I thought as I slid off the bed. Thankfully, the beautiful rose dress wasn't wrinkled and quickly fluffed out to its original state. Even the pearls in my hair seemed to have stayed in place, so I headed down the hall to join Grayson.

He was standing on the balcony looking out over the lake and didn't hear me walk into the sitting room. He would have liked the composition that his tall silhouette made against the late afternoon sky. I remembered standing next to him there on our first evening at Geilgess. Everything had seemed so perfect for one shiny moment.

I stepped out onto the balcony to join him. I couldn't think of anything to say so we just stood there for a moment in silence, looking out at the grandeur of the kingdom.

My kingdom.

Grayson broke the silence and turned to me.

"Danni, I never got the chance to tell you. I didn't know. You have to believe me, I didn't know that any of this was going to happen. I would never have put you, or Abbey, or Tyler in danger. Never."

"Grayson, it's okay." I stepped closer to him and put my hand on his arm. My heart skipped its customary beat when I looked up into his handsome face. "How could you have known that any of this would happen? The truth is, we still don't know what is going on, so we have to work with what we do know, and what we do know is that we have each other. I trust you, Grayson."

I saw his face soften with relief as his hand covered mine.

"Thank God you are okay." Unexpectedly, he pulled me to him in a hug and I relaxed into his embrace. I would like to have stayed there for a while, but in a moment he stepped back and offered his other arm.

"Are you ready?"

I nodded. It was somehow more magical than before to walk down the enchanted forest corridor on Grayson's arm. The animals seemed more animated as they scampered along behind us. How amazing it all was.

I held on to Grayson tightly as we descended the staircase into the Great Hall. Tyler, Abbey, and Grif were waiting for us to join them. Abbey started prancing with excitement when she saw me. In fact they all had strange expectant looks on their faces.

"Hi, guys. Sorry I slept so long."

Abbey suddenly let out a squeal that made me jump. Tyler and Grayson burst into laughter and even Grif smiled.

"What?" I couldn't figure out what they were up to.

"Look behind you!" Abbey finally spilled the beans.

When I turned I couldn't believe my eyes. Hanging above the massive fireplace at the end of the room was a remarkable portrait of me dressed as the Archpraelia of the Defenders. I dropped Grayson's arm and took a few steps toward it. It was uncanny and a little overwhelming to see myself in such a larger-than-life way, presiding over the great dining hall. Without a doubt, Grayson was the artist. It was done in his unique style. This must have been the project he was working on for Winnow. It was exquisite in every way, right down to the tiniest detail on the ornate ceremonial armor I was wearing. Castle Geilgess served as the backdrop high on the hill behind me. My hair was lifted in the wind along with the cape I was wearing. I looked beautiful, and noble, and brave.

I was speechless for a minute and then I turned to look at Grayson.

"Grayson, thank you. It's…it's amazing."

"You're amazing." He said quietly.

"She is indeed." Winnow came bustling in carrying mounds of food. "But she needs to eat and then she needs to return to her room to rest. Let's not forget that she is still mending."

"Oh Winnow, this looks wonderful. Thank you!" I said hurrying over to the table. I was truly hungry and

I wanted some of everything she had laid out. "I'm okay, really. I feel much better."

"For that I am thankful, Your Highness, but you still need to eat and rest properly. Tomorrow is a big day." She said as she poured us all large glasses of milk while we took our seats.

"Tomorrow?" I was intrigued and a little alarmed. "What happens tomorrow?"

"Tomorrow will take care of itself," Winnow said in her usual evasive manner, but I noticed a tightness around her mouth. She seemed more serious than usual. "Now if you'll excuse me, I have much to do." And with a quick curtsy she was gone.

For the next hour it was almost as if none of the horrible things had happened. We talked and laughed and avoided any mention of recent events. I was ravenous and managed to gobble down large quantities of food in a most unladylike manner – my beautiful dress barely escaping several mishaps. Abbey seemed like her joyful little self again, and Grif even spoke a few times and smiled a lot. I didn't want to seem vain, but I couldn't help but glance from time to time at Grayson's incredible portrait. He caught me once and smiled. I could tell that he was pleased.

We had barely polished off a decadent piece of cake for dessert when Isa scurried in, curtsied quickly, and bustled Abbey and Grif out of the room and off to bed amid a lot of pleading and groaning from Abbey.

Then it was just the three of us sitting there, dwarfed by the huge dining hall.

"Isa seems nice." I commented to break the silence.

Grayson nodded. "Abbey really likes her – and Grif, too. She's really sweet."

"And very pretty." I teased. Both boys looked uncomfortable so I thought I would change the subject.

"So what is happening tomorrow?" I asked. Grayson shook his head and scooted his chair back.

"I think Winnow has something planned, but she won't tell us what it is. We'd better get you back to bed before we all get into trouble." I hated to admit it, but I was starting to feel weary.

Both Grayson and Tyler escorted me to the door of my chambers. Tyler had been unusually quiet all evening, and saying goodnight to them both at once was awkward.

"We're just down the next hall if you need us." Tyler said.

"Thanks. I'll see you in the morning." I said as I slipped inside and closed the door. The princess suite felt very empty without them. I wandered over to the balcony and stood for a few minutes, admiring the stars in the night sky. It was hard to tell where the twinkling lights of the village ended and the stars began. It was pure magic, but weariness had set in. I retreated to my bedroom where Winnow was busy laying out a pretty nightgown. With her help, I changed and eagerly crawled into bed. I think I was asleep before my head hit the pillow.

The top step of the lost house had somehow become the landing page for my dreams, but it felt good to be here again. The dappled sunlight and warm stone was as inviting this time as when Pax had first lured me up its steps – back when he was just a laughing boy in my dreams – before all of this. Before Geilgess.

I heard a noise and turned to look back toward the overgrown fir trees that formed the hedge and kept this place a secret from the rest of the world. I hoped it was Pax. I missed him. I quickly jumped up and bounded down the steps, being careful to hop over the first one because I remembered it was wobbly.

The abandoned yard was in bad need of tending, but I quickly picked my way through the tall grass and reached the hedge in no time, turning sideways to slip through before hopping over the little trench that separated the yard from the road. I was disappointed. Pax was nowhere in sight.

I heard someone laugh back on the other side of the hedge.

"Pax. Is that you?" I chided as I shoved back through the shrubs. I froze in stunned surprise. Had I gotten turned around somehow? I was standing in the manicured yard of a lovely old Victorian-style home. The same steps and columns were there, only now they served as the entrance to a real house with a large, rambling porch and lots of windows. Its pale buttercup color and white trim was perfectly inviting.

Only happy people could live here, I thought.

A woman in gardening clothes and a large floppy hat was busy planting flowers next to the steps. She looked familiar, as did the man sitting on the porch reading a book. Neither of them saw me standing there at first. Something about the sunlight filtering in through the surrounding trees gave the whole scene a hazy, illusory quality.

"Can I help you?" The woman had turned to pick up a pot of pansies and discovered me. The man looked my way, too. I felt like I should know them both.

"I...I'm sorry. I was looking for my friend. Is this the house that once burned down?" It felt like a silly question, but I had to ask.

"I don't know." The woman didn't seem surprised by my question. "Do you, dear?"

The man on the porch wrinkled his brow and considered it for a moment.

"I really can't say," he said. "But I do think this house was here for a long time before we moved in. It's very old."

"Well, there you have it!" the woman laughed warmly. "It's older than us and that is saying something."

I couldn't help but smile back, although it made no sense...but then, it was a dream after all, right?

"Would you like to come in for some lemonade and caramel cookies?" the woman asked kindly. "I made them fresh this morning."

"Oh, no, thank you though." Part of me wanted a cookie and to see what the house looked like inside, but I was worried about Pax. And I had the nagging feeling that at any minute this dream could turn into a nightmare.

"Maybe next time, then. You're certainly welcome anytime." The woman smiled and turned back to her flowers and the man picked up his book again.

"Thanks." I turned to go back through the shrubs but stopped.

"It's beautiful."

"What, dear?" The lady asked, not really looking at me anymore as she patted the dirt around the pansies and considered her handiwork.

"The house. It's really pretty."

"Why thank you. We like it. It's home." She turned to smile at me again and I thought I caught a glimpse of a shiny key around her neck. I shivered for no reason.

"Goodbye." I said and quickly pushed through the shrubbery, stepping back over the trench and onto the road. I backed away from the hedge and looked around. I realized I didn't really know where this road was or which way to go now, and I felt sure that if I crossed back into the yard something different would be waiting there…something frightening. I wanted Pax. Where was he?

I wanted to go home.

I awoke to dappled sunlight, the smell of hot tea and scones, and no more pain in my side. I actually felt like my old self again. I knew instantly that I had regained my strength. I sat up and stretched happily, soaking in the beauty around me. It dawned on me that I knew almost nothing about Geilgess. Who had designed this magnificent castle and this spectacular room? I had to remember to ask Winnow for a history lesson.

I made my way to the table with the breakfast tray and poured myself a cup of tea. As I took a bite of the scone, I sensed it. Something was different this morning. First of all, Winnow was missing. She was usually bustling about or fussing over me. I wondered what she was up to. She said today would be a big day. What did that mean?

I finished off my cup of tea and tilted my head back to look at the lovely painted ceiling with its puffy clouds. It really was exquisite. And then I did something silly. I did a little pirouette and danced across the floor. The dainty nightgown I was wearing flowed gracefully around me. I had watched Mariela dance many times and then practiced the steps secretly on my own. I guess every little girl wants to be a ballerina or a princess, even though I had never minded being the tomboy either.

I stopped twirling in front of the swan tapestry and stood for a long time, looking up at the swan's beautiful face and noble expression. There was a message woven into the threads of her eyes and I completely understood it. As lovely as this room was, and as pretty as the ball gowns had been, I had been dressed in stable-boy britches when I truly became the Princess of Geilgess.

I took a step back and did a little curtsy to the swan. I was starting to feel antsy. I couldn't get dressed yet, but I could at least start on my hair, so I headed to the dressing table. That's when I saw my clothes. I hadn't noticed them before, but my pajamas along with my hoodie and sneakers had all been carefully and purposely placed on the dressing table chair. I hadn't seen my old clothes in a while, so they had to be there for a reason.

I wasn't going to wait for Winnow to arrive with an explanation – something was wrong. I needed to find the others. It only took a few minutes for me to get dressed this time and as soon as I got my sneakers tied, I was running down the hallway. I burst into the sitting room just as Tyler, Grayson, and Abbey came in the other door. They were dressed in their regular clothes, too. Grayson was carrying Abbey, who was wearing her pink pajamas, and had obviously been crying.

"What's going on?" My voice stuck in my throat. It had to be bad, whatever it was.

"We don't know." Tyler looked grim. "Isa took Grif from the nursery this morning. We don't know where she took him. Our old clothes were laid out for us."

"We need to find Winnow." I tried to control my voice as I pushed past them into the enchanted forest hallway. I had no idea where Winnow always disappeared to, but we could start with the side door in the great dining hall. I was only vaguely aware of the animation that surrounded us in the corridor as I moved quickly to the end of the hall and started down the grand staircase. I did steal one glance at my portrait over the fireplace as I hurried down the steps. We didn't have to look long for Winnow because she entered from the servant's door at the far end of the room just as we reached the bottom.

"Winnow!" I ran to her, but stopped when I realized she was carrying Abbey's pink backpack which appeared to be heavy and full.

"Winnow. What is going on?" My voice trembled because I could see the tension on her face.

"Your Highness." Before I knew what was happening Winnow seemed to be losing her balance. Thankfully, Tyler was by her side immediately and helped her into one of the large chairs at the end of the table. I quickly grabbed the backpack and knelt so that I could see her face clearly.

"Winnow. Are you okay?" It was distressing to see her like this. She had always been our rock. She nodded and tried to get up but Tyler and I kept her safely in the chair.

"I'm so sorry, Princess. The news has been difficult." Winnow was quickly composing herself.

"What news, Winnow? Please, tell us what is happening."

"The High Counsel was attacked last night."

"What?" I gasped. "Are Pax and Kyna all right?"

"I do not know." Winnow's voice was still a little shaky, but she swallowed hard and continued. "It happened at the final session."

"The Queen? Is she all right?" I could barely bring myself to ask.

Winnow nodded. "Yes, the Imperial Majesty has been moved to a safe location; that much we do know. And that is what we must do for you now. You are all to return to your home of origin at once. It is for your own safety. It will be a difficult journey, I fear. We must get you on your way quickly."

"Winnow. We can't just leave." I was completely confused. I almost told her that Geilgess is our home now, but then I grasped what saying that would mean.

"Yes, you must and you will." Winnow said gravely. "You have no choice. It is an Imperial Order. Arthmael is preparing a group of Defenders to take you to the edge of the Sovereign Forest at once." Winnow stood up with renewed determination. "We must hurry."

I stood up, too, but I was far from ready to leave – although just the thought of going home was filling me with a kind of relief and elation.

"Winnow, we can't just leave you here. What if Geilgess is attacked? I am the Princess. I should stay and help. Tyler and Grayson and Abbey should go ahead."

"We're not going anywhere without you." Tyler said sternly.

Winnow suddenly broke into such a bright smile that it shocked us all. She almost looked like a different person. She took me completely by surprise as she cupped my face in her hands.

"There now. You said it." She held my face gently and I was mystified by her proud expression.

"What, Winnow?" I was confused. "I don't understand."

"You said that you are the Princess. You finally believe it." She announced, and in a most un-Winnow-like move, she leaned over and kissed my forehead.

"And now you must believe this, too," she continued with great conviction. "All will be well. Geilgess will remain, but the forests will grow quiet for a time. That is why we must hurry if we are to get you home. You must all return together as you came."

I felt tears pushing at my eyes, but I tried to keep them under control.

"But what about Grif? What will happen to him?" I asked.

"Grif and Arthmael have formed a powerful bond and Arthmael has pledged to be his guardian. He and Isa will see to it that Grif has everything he needs."

"But we didn't get to say goodbye." Abbey sobbed. My heart broke for her because she was losing another person in her life. Winnow walked over to Grayson and stroked Abbey's hair.

"Well then, Miss Abigail, it means this isn't goodbye."

Abbey seemed comforted by that and she nodded.

"Now," Winnow returned to her brisk efficient self. "We must hurry. This way." She headed toward the side door that opened into the Hall of Defenders. I exchanged questioning glances with Tyler and Grayson. Tyler shook his head and Grayson scowled.

There was no right answer. We didn't know what else to do but follow her.

I turned as we left the Great Hall to glance back at my portrait and the massive tapestry, with its dense forest and mystical orbs. I had no idea if I would ever see this place again. I couldn't fight the tears any longer as we headed down the corridor. The exquisite statues of Defenders saluted us as we hurried to keep up with Winnow.

We entered the same winding stairwell that I had used on the night I left to find Kyna. Now, small slits in the stone wall provided just enough daylight for us to make our way to the bottom. The large door to the courtyard was still open wide and we emerged into the sunlight to see four Defenders on horseback. Arthmael was one of them, and he looked as striking as the first time I saw him with his long braids and cape. He didn't dismount this time, but literally scooped me off the ground to sit in front of him. Grayson, Tyler, and Abbey were quickly picked up, too, and the horses pranced with energy.

"Princess, we must hurry." Arthmael's voice was commanding.

This was all happening too fast.

"Winnow!" I reached down to her and probably would have fallen off if Arthmael hadn't been holding me so tightly. Winnow rushed over and wrapped something around my wrist. I couldn't see what it was for the tears.

"Thank you." I sobbed, grabbing her hand. "For everything."

"Remember who you are, Your Highness." She said ardently. "Remember who you are."

"Now go!" She commanded Arthmael, and within seconds we were galloping across the bridge at breakneck speed. I could just make out the road as it started to appear before us, but the landscape was a liquid blur as I wept uncontrollably and clutched Arthmael's arm. I managed one last look back at the castle before it vanished from sight behind a hill.

CHAPTER 14

It had been hours since the Defenders had deposited us at the entrance to the Sovereign Forest. Our goodbyes had been brief, ending with the solemn salute of the Defenders before they galloped away, swathed in a sense of urgency. They were needed elsewhere. Long after they disappeared from sight, we had stood silently watching as the road they left on disappeared until finally we were left staring at an empty field and some rolling hills. We had walked for a long time in near silence since then.

The Sovereign Forest was no doubt the most beautiful place we had been so far, but it was hard to appreciate its grandeur. We were all dealing with the grief of leaving Geilgess in our own way, and silence seemed to offer the most solace. Abbey would occasionally ask for some water, but she didn't want any of the food that Winnow had so carefully packed for us. Winnow had thought of everything. Even our original plastic water bottles had been filled, and my flashlight had been tucked into the zippered pouch of Abbey's pink backpack, which Tyler was wearing at the moment.

It was easy to see how the Sovereign Forest got its name. The trees were massive and ancient and majestic, and as we walked, our route was revealed to us by the lifting of their bowed limbs. Once we passed, the limbs bowed again to conceal where we had been. The sunlight seemed to frolic happily around us as it filtered through the leaves overhead. At times the whole forest seemed to dance, reminding me of the enchanted corridor outside my rooms at Geilgess.

Grayson seemed lost in thought, his scowl more prominent than usual. My own thoughts bounced around uncontrollably as I replayed the events of the last week on a continual loop. No matter how hard I tried, I couldn't make sense of it. It seemed like we had been working a puzzle only to reach the end with several pieces missing.

I gently touched the bracelet Winnow had slipped onto my wrist as we said goodbye. It was made of braided ribbons with one lovely charm dangling from its center – a crowned swan – just like the one in my room at Geilgess.

"Remember who you are," she had said, but I wasn't so sure anymore. My heart ached to think of leaving her without knowing if she would be safe.

There was a movement ahead of us on the path and we all stopped in our tracks. Abbey caught her breath, but didn't make another sound. A tree limb had lifted to reveal a stunning white deer standing in our way. He was very large with impressive antlers and beautiful eyes. He didn't seemed startled by us at all, but stood looking at us with a gaze that was almost thoughtful. He remained completely still for several minutes, creating quite a picture for us, his white coat glowing in the sun. He was altogether radiant.

Before Grayson could stop her, Abbey took a couple of steps forward and held out her hand.

"Hello."

With amazing gracefulness and power, the deer turned and leapt high into the air and was gone, swallowed up by the forest foliage.

"Now that's not something you see every day." Tyler wasn't being glib, he was quite serious.

"I've never seen a white deer before." I agreed.

"He was pretty." Abbey nodded. It was as if the white deer had lifted our veil of sorrow and we all seemed a little happier as we moved forward. Abbey hitched a ride with Grayson and promptly fell asleep on his shoulder. I wondered how much further we would have to walk before we reached the place of convergence. I kept thinking about Kyna and how she seemed to have summoned one on her own, and I wondered if I really had the power to do it, too, or if I had just dreamed it. Either way, it was a terrifying thought.

The day was growing late before we stopped for something to eat. We settled on a spot at the base of one of the immense trees. Its large gnarled roots created a lovely little niche for a picnic and a place to lean back and rest. We could hear water running nearby, and upon investigation found a delightful babbling brook with moss covered rocks and ice-cold water that felt so good on my face. After we filled our water bottles, we made our way back to the tree and demolished most of the food Winnow had packed for us, and then the weariness set in.

"It's getting kind of late," Tyler said, glancing up at the waning sunlight. "Do you think we should camp here for the night and get a fresh start in the morning?"

Grayson nodded. "I notice the trees aren't moving. I think maybe we are supposed to."

"I think you are right." I agreed. "Besides, I don't know about you guys, but I could use the rest." I really was exhausted.

"How is your side? Does it hurt?" I appreciated the concern on Tyler's face. It did ache a little, but I didn't want to complain.

"I'm good. Thanks."

And then we did what campers have always done.

We told stories.

Tyler told about getting lost with his scout troupe only to find out in the morning they were hunkered down and waiting for help only twenty yards from the parking lot. I talked about my dad making me eat worms on a survival camping trip we took when I was seven, which resulted in my decision to become a vegetarian.

"Eeew!" Abbey's face cracked us all up.

"Well, that explains why there was never any meat in the meals at Geilgess." Tyler laughed.

"And you didn't really miss it, now, did you?" I asked defensively.

"No," he acknowledged, "The food was pretty amazing. Which is not to say that I'm not going to raid the fridge the minute I get home." We all laughed at that.

"What about you, Gray?" Tyler asked. "Any camping nightmares?"

"We never really did much camping. Well, Terry and I would put up a tent in the backyard sometimes." There was pain in Grayson's voice and on his face so I quickly changed the subject.

"Okay, Abbey." I tried to lighten the mood. "This is your first camping trip, so you get to tell us a story." I could tell that she was a little nervous about being in the woods at night so giving her something to do to occupy her thoughts seemed like a good idea.

"What kind of story?" She asked, wrinkling her nose and pushing up her glasses.

"Whatever kind of story you want to tell." I encouraged her. "Maybe you can tell us about one of the adventures that happened at your dollhouse." Abbey's face lit up with excitement and for the next hour or so she was the center of attention and she ate it up. Her story was so convoluted that we couldn't follow it, but she was having so much fun that we gave her our full attention, although the guys kept interrupting to give her a hard time about the characters, which included a unicorn, a rabbit, and, of course, a princess.

I watched as Grayson's face softened and his worried brow relaxed while he listened to Abbey. Even without the castle clothes, he was princely and completely gorgeous. I loved to see him laugh. I looked away from him quickly when I saw Tyler watching me.

The story kept Abbey busy as the woods started to grow dark around us, but she was quickly running out of steam – and story ideas.

"Abbey, look." I interrupted her. As the night approached, the entire forest was filling up with fireflies. It was a marvelous sight. We were surrounded by their twinkling yellow glow as they danced around us and sailed up into the treetops.

"Wow." Abbey was enraptured.

"Here," Grayson pulled her into his lap and we all scooted back to lean against the base of the ancient tree and watch the firefly show. The darkness came quickly and the night air was cool, but not uncomfortable. I covered Abbey with my hoodie and she snuggled against my arm. It felt safe to have Grayson on one side and Tyler on the other. Abbey yawned and it was catching. I yawned, too.

"Why don't the two of you get some sleep?" Tyler said, taking charge. He had pulled the backpack to his side and taken out the flashlight. "Gray and I will take turns standing watch."

I was too tired to argue and I noticed that Abbey was already sound asleep.

"We have to stay together," I cautioned sleepily. "We don't know when the convergence will happen."

Tyler moved so that I could lean against him. His warmth felt good.

"We've got this, Danni. Get some rest."

My eyes felt heavy and the twinkling fireflies became blurry. As I gave into sleep, I wondered if the beautiful white deer was somewhere nearby, watching us.

The moon on the horizon was huge and so bright that the fields behind where the house had once stood glowed an eerie silver, causing the abandoned swing set to stand out like an abstract painting. The top step was a little chilly so I sat cross-legged, watching the moon inch its way into the sky. I was so happy and relieved to turn and find Pax sitting beside me.

"Pax! You're okay!" I hugged him tightly and he hugged me back. His crystalline eyes were glowing as brightly as the moon.

"Is Kyna...," I could barely bring myself to ask. "Is everyone okay?"

Pax took my hand and looked down at it for a moment. I was terrified of what he might say, but he nodded.

"Everyone is okay. For now."

I breathed a sigh of relief.

"I was afraid I wouldn't get to say goodbye to you." My voice broke.

"Why would you want to?" He spoke quietly and his eyes met mine, flashing with intensity as he searched my face with a penetrating gaze. There was something so compelling about Pax. Even though he wasn't traditionally handsome, he was quite beautiful to look at. Almost like a statue come to life. The moonlight only accentuated the perfect lines of his face.

"I don't!" I stammered. "I just thought...I mean, I don't know how this works."

Pax nodded. "The most important thing right now is that you and the others are safe." He paused for a moment, sighed heavily, and tightened his grip on my hand. "There are dark forces at work, Princess."

"Can I help? Tell me what I can do, Pax. What is going on? Why does everything have to be such a mystery?"

"I'm sorry, Danni. I don't have all the answers. I only see things in distorted bits and pieces." His jaw tightened as he spoke. "It's up to the Imperial Majesty and the High Counsel to decide whether or not what I see has any significance. What I do know is that you are in danger and that I will do everything I can to protect you." His tone sent shivers up my spine. He released my hand as I took a deep breath and looked around, wondering if I would see this place again.

"The last time I was here looking for you, there was a house," I said quietly. "And there was a woman planting flowers and a man on the porch. I felt like I should know them both, but I couldn't quite figure out who they were."

Pax smiled at me and his eyes did that flickering thing.

"Perhaps this place is your threshold of possibility, Princess. What happens here is up to you."

Was he telling me that I had imagined a future here – or a past? I looked around and tried to picture the house again, but I could only catch a fleeting glimpse in my mind. I tried to remember the faces of the man and woman, too, but I couldn't quite see them anymore.

When I turned back to ask Pax what he meant, he had vanished. I was alone on the top step as everything faded into a silvery soft-focus.

"Danni!" Tyler's voice penetrated my consciousness and I struggled to get up, only to realize that he was pulling a wet limb off of me. Grayson and Abbey were getting up next to me. It was raining hard, and it took a second for me to grasp where we were. The flashlight, laying a few feet away, was giving off just enough light for me to make out that we were back in the abandoned swimming hole in the woods behind our houses. Thunder rumbled in the distance.

"You okay?" He asked, and I nodded.

"We must have fallen asleep when it happened," Grayson sounded as stunned as I was. I knew he was referring to the convergence. "The last thing I remembered was us talking," he said to Tyler.

"Yeah, me too." Tyler sounded unnerved.

"Are we home?" Abbey asked sleepily.

"I think we might be, Sparkle Butt." Tyler shot us both a wary glance. "You guys are going to stay here while I go check it out, okay?" He grabbed one of the vines hanging down the bank and was halfway up before we could say anything.

"I'll be right back." He called down at us as he heaved himself over the rim and disappeared into the darkness. There was an awkward silence as we stood there getting soaked. Grayson picked up Abbey and covered her with the hoodie.

"He should have taken the flashlight." I noted.

"He'll be okay," Grayson sounded confident. "He knows his way around here." I just hoped "here" was where we thought it was, but I didn't say that.

Tyler was back in just a couple of minutes. He swung down the vine and landed with a splash of mud next to me. I could tell he was excited.

"They're there. The houses. All of them. They're fine. We're home."

For a moment we stood there looking at each other with rivulets of rain running down our faces. A rumble of thunder sounded in the far off distance. The storm was moving away.

We are really home.

I waited until Grayson had lifted Abbey up to Tyler and then quickly climbed up after her. Wet weeds slapped my legs on the short path out of the woods. With the storm gone, the sky was growing a little lighter, indicating that morning would soon be arriving. Across the field I could see Granddad's house and Grayson's house next door, with the lights on just like he had left them. We stopped at the big boulder, unsure of what to do next.

"Maybe we can get together later and talk." Grayson suggested. "I need to get Abbey inside. She's soaked."

"Sounds good." Tyler nodded and then looked at me. "If anything is wrong, if anything has changed, we'll be right next door."

"Okay." I agreed.

We crossed the field quickly and quietly, and before I knew it, I was climbing up the steps to the deck and slipping back through the sliding glass doors into my room. Everything was just as I had left it, only the clock now read 5:02. Had we really only been away for 45 minutes?

I couldn't tell if I was shivering from the wet clothes or shock, but I knew what I had to do. I hastily dried myself, making as little noise as possible. I didn't want to wake Granddad and Myra. I pulled on my favorite sweats, wrapped my hair in a towel, and then rummaged through the desk drawer for a pad of sticky notes and the felt pen that I had seen there earlier. I needed to write down everything. The Queen had said that we would forget Geilgess as time went by. I wasn't going to let that happen.

I had an idea.

I went into my closet, pulled on the light, and gently pushed my clothes to one side so that I could get into the recessed area. No one would be apt to look here. I pasted the front wall of the closet with sticky notes and started writing feverishly. I wrote down everything I could remember. Names, the rooms at the castle, descriptions of the Defenders, the corridors, the armory, the names of the forests, the strange stone meeting room with five chairs, the fortress, the Dragon Prince, the people that had fallen under his spell, the swans, the dreams, the infirmary, the white flowered trees at the lake, the convergences, the white deer. Everything. I ran out of sticky notes at one point and tiptoed into Granddad's den in the next room to find more.

I was exhausted by the time I finished, and it looked like I had wallpapered the front and side wall of the closet. A knock at my bedroom door brought me back to the present. I quickly hopped out of the closet, slid the door shut behind me and opened the bedroom door with a yawn. It was Granddad dressed in a robe and slippers, and carrying a large cup of coffee.

"Hey young'un! Good morning!"

"Hey Granddad!" I threw my arms around him, trying not to spill his coffee. I was so happy to see him.

"You are up early. Did you get any sleep? That was some storm we had last night, wasn't it?"

"Yeah, it was pretty intense." I swallowed hard and tried to keep my face under control. He gave me a quizzical look.

"I was watching the early news and there may have been a tornado sighting in the next county, but I don't think there was any damage. Here," he proffered the coffee cup. "This is for you."

I accepted it gratefully. "Thanks, Granddad. I can really use it."

He laughed. "You'll eventually figure out which time zone you are in." He started to turn and then remembered something.

"Oh, I am supposed to tell you that 'come-as-you-are-Sunday-pancake-breakfast' is served at zero eight hundred hours. You don't want to be late," he laughed again. "Myra's pancakes are a thing of beauty."

He started to turn again and remembered something else. "Oh, and we leave for church at exactly zero nine thirty hours. Myra teaches Sunday School."

"Thanks, Granddad. I'll be ready." I wanted to hug him again, but he was already heading down the hallway with a wave.

"Best pancakes in the state of Georgia, "he called back over his shoulder.

He wasn't kidding. Myra's pancakes were out of this world – chock full of pecans and oozing with butter and syrup.

"Those pecans are from my mom's house," Myra said. She was so cute puttering around the kitchen in her robe with curlers in her hair. Obviously "come-as-you-are-pancake-breakfast" was exactly that.

"Myra, these are the best pancakes I've ever eaten!" I said and I meant it. What I couldn't tell them was how strange it felt to be sitting at their dining room table when only a few days ago, I was eating in the great dining hall at Geilgess. It didn't help that

Granddad kept looking at me curiously over the top of his newspaper.

"Your mom called again last night." His statement took me so off guard that I dropped my fork with a clatter.

"Sorry."

"She really needs to be reminded about the time difference, honey." Myra fussed as she started putting bowls into the dishwasher.

"I don't have to go back, do I?" I could tell that it wasn't what either of them was expecting to hear from me.

"No." Granddad laid his paper down and studied me intensely. "She didn't mention it, but I do think she is feeling bad about everything."

"Well, she should!" Myra admonished from the kitchen. "But that's okay, we definitely got the good end of this arrangement!" She winked at me.

I loved Myra for having my back and got up to help her with the dishes just as the wall phone rang. She answered it and immediately went off down the hallway chatting excitedly. I could feel Granddad watching me as I cleaned up.

"You sure you're okay, young'un?" He finally asked. I didn't want to lie to him. I wasn't really sure how I was. Part of me felt like I was on autopilot. Myra came back into the room in a bustle and I was glad that I didn't have to answer.

"That was Susan from up the street. She said there's someone moving into the Monroe house today."

"Really?" Granddad was interested in this new information and, thankfully, forgot about his question to me.

"Yes, she's going to see what she can find out about them." Myra seemed thrilled with the news. "Do you think we should invite them to church?"

"Well, honey, don't you think it's a little soon if they are just moving in?"

"It's never too soon to invite someone to church," Myra admonished, "but you are probably right. Maybe we can take a casserole over this afternoon. I think I have one in the freezer I can heat up."

"That sounds like a good plan." Granddad winked at me, pushed his chair back, and glanced at his watch. "You about ready, young'un?"

"Almost," I smiled. "I just need to brush my teeth and change shoes."

"Well, let's meet back here in forty-five." He got up and herded Myra toward the stairs.

After they left I stood for a minute in the solitude of the room with a thousand thoughts running through my mind. I finally turned and caught sight of myself in one of the decorative mirrors on the wall. I was wearing a dress that Kim had given me when she cleaned out her closet last year, my dad's key was secure at my neck, and Winnow's ribbon bracelet was still wrapped around my wrist.

Remember who you are.

I wasn't sure who that was anymore. The only thing I was certain of was that I wanted – no, I needed – to see Grayson.

I practically flew out the front door. The sprinklers were watering the flower beds beside the house, but I didn't care. I hopped across the mulch, losing a flip flop on the way. I kicked the other one off. The garage door to Grayson's house was open and I ran right in, not sure what I was going to do if he wasn't there.

He was.

He was hunched over his art table and it looked like he had been drawing since early morning. There were pages and pages of sketches all around him. When he saw me, he stood up and I ran right into his arms. If it surprised him, he didn't let on. He just folded me into an embrace, and held me tightly. I wanted to stay there forever.

He gently ran his fingers through my hair and leaned close.

"Are you okay?" He asked softly.

I forced myself to step back.

"I'm okay. Everything just seems strange. How are you?"

He glanced around at his work and handed one of his sketches to me. His drawings were amazing. They were just quick sketches, but he had captured everything about Geilgess in a minimum of strokes. I had to swallow back tears when I saw his rendering of Winnow. I missed her so much already.

"I've been trying to get it all down, you know? So that we don't forget."

"I've been writing stuff down, too." I said.

"Good."

"How is Abbey?"

"She's okay. She filled Dad's ears full of stories at breakfast, but he just thinks it's more of her imaginary friend stuff."

"Maybe that's for the best."

"I don't know." He shook his head. "She's so fragile right now."

I reached out and took his hand.

"We'll figure this out."

He nodded, and suddenly being there felt very awkward. I pulled my hand away and changed the subject.

"How's Tyler doing?"

"He went home, but he said he'd stop back by tonight. Maybe we can talk then."

"Sounds good," I said, backing away. "I have to go, we're leaving for church in just a few minutes. Will you be there?" I tried to sound as casual as possible.

"I have to get ready for work, but Abbey and Dad may go."

"Where do you work?" I don't know why I was surprised that he had a job, but I was.

"At the Comic Depot in Hadley. Just a few hours a week. It helps pay for all of this," he motioned to his paints and brushes. "Plus I get to see a lot of great art. You should come by some time."

"Cool. Well, okay. I'd better go. See you later then." I turned to leave when a large piece of sketch paper near the front of the garage caught my eye. The wind had probably blown it into the front corner. I stooped to pick it up and stopped in my tracks when I saw what was on it.

I turned to look at Grayson. He was watching me -- staring at me strangely.

"Grayson, when did you do this?"

He walked over and took it from my hands.

"A couple of months ago, I guess. I had forgotten about it. It didn't seem to fit with the rest of them."

It wouldn't.

He handed the sketch back to me and as I looked at it again, I felt a wave of terror pass over me. The drawing was set in front of Malvern High School. The "Go Mavericks" banner was hanging on the brick buildings just like when I first arrived. Several school buses were drawn off to the side, but the focal point of the picture was a guy standing on the curb in front of the school. He appeared to be waiting on someone. Even in a sketch, his identity was unmistakable. He was the Dragon Prince complete with spiked blonde hair, and dark, rimmed eyes – only now he was sporting a leather jacket and a dangling earring to go along with his cruel, sensuous smile. And the most terrifying part was that he was staring right off the page at me, like I was the one he was waiting for.

ACKNOWLEDGEMENTS

I thank God for all the wonderful people who have offered their support and encouragement during the writing of this book:

To my friend, Sandy Sallee, thank you for being the best cheerleader ever! You are such a blessing. Ooh sa sa sa!

My deepest gratitude to Jennifer Winchester and Katie Cline for being so completely fabulous and willing to help! You have touched and inspired me with your kindness and generosity.

A very special thank you to Linda, Megan, and Todd Kuhar for doing such an amazing job of capturing the beautiful cover photo that brought my vision of the princess to life.

To my talented friend, Alfred Ramirez, thank you so much for the marvelous illustrations and conceptual artwork. You are the best!

To my gifted editor, Amber Harrelson-Williams, thank you, thank you, thank you from the bottom of my heart for being so fantastic to work with! I could not have done it without you.

Loads of love to my sister, Pam Johnson, and my BFF, Tricia Lindsay-Ramirez. Thank you for your guidance and for always believing in me.

And a huge thanks to Mallory Rock for creating such a stunning cover design and for all the brilliant finishing touches! Mallory, you are awesome!

ABOUT THE AUTHOR

Ariel Lucas started writing as a teenager for her high school newspaper and wrote her first fiction story on a cross country flight to San Francisco. Maybe it was the star-studded night sky or just the altitude, but she was totally hooked.

Her love of great stories and dynamic characters eventually drew her to the theatre and a career in performing arts. She has studied at Miami Acting Studio, and is the author of several stories for children.

She currently resides in beautiful Western North Carolina. *The Princess of Windswept* is her first YA novel.

Made in the USA
Columbia, SC
14 April 2022